HENRY GALLANT AND THE GREAT SHIP

H. Peter Alesso

THE HENRY GALLANT SAGA

Midshipman Henry Gallant in Space © 2013
Lieutenant Henry Gallant © 2014
<u>Henry Gallant and the *Warrior*</u> © 2015
Commander Henry Gallant © 2016
Captain Henry Gallant © 2019
Commodore Henry Gallant © 2020
Henry Gallant and the Great Ship © 2020
Rear Admiral Henry Gallant © 2021

Other Novels by H. Peter Alesso

Captain Hawkins © 2016
Dark Genius © 2017
Youngblood © 2018

HENRY GALLANT AND THE GREAT SHIP

H. Peter Alesso
hpeteralesso.com

© 2020 H. Peter Alesso

This is a work of fiction. All characters, dialog, and events portrayed in this book are fictional, and any resemblance to real people or incidents is purely coincidental.

All rights reserved.

No part of this publication may be reproduced, stored in a retrieval system, or transmitted, in any form or by any means without prior permission in writing from:

VSL Publications
Pleasanton, CA 94566

Edition 1.00
ISBN-13: 979-8698735410

H. PETER ALESSO

∞

To those who have ever worn the uniform,

Thank you for your service.

United Planets—Task Force 34
Captain Henry Gallant
    2 Spacecraft Carriers – Starfighter Space Wing – Lieutenant Rob Ryan
        Constellation
            36 Viper I – Squadron 6
            48 Viper II – Squadron 8
            6 Hawkeye – Squadron 10
        Courageous
            36 Viper I – Squadron 7
            48 Viper II – Squadron 9
            6 Hawkeye – Squadron 11
    3 Battlecruisers – *Indefatigable, Inflexible, Invincible*
        12 Cruisers
        48 Destroyers
        2 Stealth Recon – *Warrior, Invidia*
        12 Auxiliary Support Ship

Marines
Major James Steward
    1st Marine Raider Battalion

Chameleon
    The Great Ship
    Asteroid Fortresses – A B C D
        4 Asteroid Battle Stations
        24 Asteroid Missile Batteries

Titan—Raiders
    6 Individual Squadrons each 1 cruiser and 6 destroyers

Titan—Battle Fleet
Admiral Zzey
    2 Spacecraft Carriers – *Vampiri, Valkyrie*
       Starfighter Space Wing
          72 Fighters
          72 Bombers
          8 Reconnaissance
    2 Dreadnought
    6 Battlecruisers
  36 Cruisers
    88 Destroyers
    88 Auxiliary Support Ships

CONTENTS

Chapter 1 An Unfortunate Turn of Events
Chapter 2 Speak Softly
Chapter 3 Kate Mahoney
Chapter 4 Gold Braid
Chapter 5 Puzzled
Chapter 6 Convoy
Chapter 7 Showmanship
Chapter 8 Search
Chapter 9 A Sitting Duck
Chapter 10 The Lad
Chapter 11 The Lie Inside the Lie
Chapter 12 Prey for Us
Chapter 13 Walkabout
Chapter 14 The Halo Effect
Chapter 15 Ryan and Lorelei
Chapter 16 A Spark in the Dark
Chapter 17 Wakeup
Chapter 18 Pivot
Chapter 19 Strike 1
Chapter 20 Fallout
Chapter 21 Jetpack
Chapter 22 Strike 2
Chapter 23 Ghost Signal
Chapter 24 Strike 3

Chapter 25 Debrief
Chapter 26 Fugazi
Chapter 27 Yes, We Can
Chapter 28 Zzey
Chapter 29 Send in the Marines
Chapter 30 Battleline
Chapter 31 Phantoms
Chapter 32 Duel
Chapter 33 Death to the Beast
Chapter 34 The Curtain Falls
Chapter 35 Everything Ends
Chapter 36 Buttons and Bows

CHAPTER 1

An Unfortunate Turn of Events

As soon as the morning watch settled in, Captain Henry Gallant walked onto the *Constellation's* bridge. The Officer-of-the-Deck rose and vacated the command chair without speaking. The voyage had lasted long enough for the crew to become accustomed to his routine. Habitually, during the first minutes of the day, he examined the ship's vital operational parameters from his bedside monitor before going into CIC for a detailed task force sitrep. Blips from the combat space patrol (CSP) were visible on the main viewer. The speakers broadcast communication traffic from distant Hawkeyes. Once he had satisfied himself that all was as it should be, he appeared on the bridge and assessed the more mundane needs for the day. The OOD handed him a list of completed tasks and those that demanded his approval. During this activity, he was lost in contemplation, and no one dared interrupt his train of thought.

Only after dictating his orders for the day

did he relax and give a word of encouragement to the OOD. Then he disappeared below decks for his daily walkabout, where he gauged the temperament of the crew. The hour exercise through the spacecraft carrier allowed him to maintain his fitness. This ritual was the most efficient use of his time since it also allowed him to observe ongoing maintenance and repair activities. On the one hand, the number of administrative duties clamoring for his attention limited his time; on the other, keeping in sync with his ship's pulse was vital to making good decisions. It brought a faint smile to his lips when he resolved to shift more of the clerical burden onto his XO. Margret Fletcher had a talent for paperwork and was known for her no-nonsense adherence to the regs. Even though he overloaded her of late, she had responded with her usual zeal.

As he passed through compartment after compartment, he dictated audio notes into his comm pin about items that needed attention. He marched along the corridors and stepped through the open hatches, ever mindful of the crew's attention. Although immersed in his process, the crew discerned that his military instincts were on full alert. He would notice the slightest failure of attention to detail as the men and women went about their jobs. Occasionally, he heard a laugh or good-natured ribbing. That was well. A crew that could laugh while working would faithfully execute their duties.

He enjoyed the sameness of each day; it reassured him that his world remained rational.

It had been two days since the *Constellation* had poked her nose into the Ross star system. Gallant congratulated himself on making the deployment from Earth so rapidly. It had been a long and arduous two-month grind, but Task Force 34 was finally ready to relieve Task Force 31 as guardian of this system.

He shifted his mind back to the disturbing initial surveillance reports that had perplexed him for the last twenty-four hours. Task Force 31 was not visible, which by itself, wasn't alarming. A planetary body might block their light, though they weren't responding to radio signals either. Again, they might be on the other side of the star, and the speed of light wasn't being accommodating. Another calculation percolated into his consciousness. He had sent Hawkeyes out on a sweep of the system. So far, nothing was amiss, but there was confusing radio chatter from the planets indicating that some horrific event had occurred recently.

Gallant returned to the bridge in time to review the latest recon update. None of the information was reassuring. He noticed an anomaly in the data that prickled the hairs on the back of his neck. Though the statistics were mysteriously thin and precariously riddled with contaminated inconsistencies, they were coaxing him toward a disturbing conclusion. He worried his premonition might be correct and ordered the CIC to conduct an AI simulation analysis. It wasn't long before Commander Fletcher stepped onto the bridge.

"Good morning, Captain," she said. Then with

a frown, she added, "I have the results."

Gallant spun in his command chair and cast a concerned eye on her.

She held a tablet by two fingers out in front of her as if she had found it in a vat of something vile.

"Morning XO," said Gallant, taking the device. Swiping through the screens, he absorbed the information while his heartbeat rose. He wanted to remain calm to reinforce his reputation as imperturbable. He didn't want Fletcher or anyone else to suspect that he could lose his composure. But he was bursting to rush into CIC. He wanted to review the raw data to verify that it was accurate, but he knew that the analysts would have been meticulous in developing this report.

She interrupted his concentration. "You were right, sir."

"Ha—h'm," he said, clearing his throat. He took a deep breath and forced himself to appear relaxed.

Fletcher shook her head and prodded, "Looks like an enormous debris field—possibly with escape pods."

She pointed to the area spread deep throughout the star system's heart, halfway between planets Bravo and Charlie. The OOD and the chief of the watch inched closer, craning their necks to get a peek at the tablet.

Gallant recalled the disturbing image of the original data. Understanding flooded over him. He visualized what must have taken place, and it took an enormous effort to suppress his emotions. She scowled. "No sign of Task Force 31."

Still, he didn't respond.

She muttered, "That doesn't necessarily mean..."

Everyone on the bridge gazed expectantly at him.

Like a father who returns home to find his front door smashed open, he ordered, "OOD, open a channel to all ships."

A moment later, the OOD reported, "Channel open to all ships, Commodore."

"To all ships, this is Commodore Gallant; set general quarters, assume formation diamond 4.4."

"Aye aye, sir," came the response from each ship.

The task force split into four strike forces. Captain Jackson of the *Courageous* led the first strike force designated 34.1. It was followed one light hour behind by 34.2 and 34.3, led by Captain Hernandez of the *Indefatigable* and Captain Chu of the *Inflexible*, respectively. They kept a light-hour separation from each other. Finally, Gallant led *Constellation* and *Invincible* in 34.4, another light hour behind the rest. The cruisers and destroyers were split amongst the strike forces. The dispersed strike forces looked like a baseball diamond with the *Constellation* at home plate.

It took several hours to complete the maneuver. Satisfied that the ships were sufficiently far apart for the majority to survive a blast from the Great Ship's super-laser, he ordered, "Task Force change course to 030 Mark 2, all ahead full."

Gallant waited anxiously on the bridge for the entire twenty-four hours it took for the task force to crawl across the Ross star system. Some telltale blips appeared on the scope interspersed within a belt of asteroids. When they were finally close enough, they saw the remains of many half-dead ships. They began picking up distress signals of countless escape pods. Officers and watch-standers on the bridge stared at the viewscreen, trying to glimpse the wreckage.

Gallant's eye estimated the number of blips. They could only be the remnants of Task Force 31. It was worse than he imagined—a terrible loss of life.

"OOD, prepare med-techs. Send the search and rescue teams to recover the escape pod survivors."

The initial action report was sent by the senior surviving officer, Captain Raymond. It was sketchy. It couldn't be called a 'battle' report since not a single ship of the task force had fired a shot.

After a brief visit to *Constellation's* sickbay, the officer reported to Gallant's stateroom.

Raymond was not quite fifty, but his balding head, sunken eyes, and beaked nose made him appear older. His long black mustache with grey flecks drooped, making him appear to frown. His uniform was in tatters, and he had several bandaged injuries that had been tended to by the ship's surgeon. His thickset body was powerful, but he stood slumped over, pain etched across his face.

"That's the scorched wreck of my ship, the *Dauntless*," said Captain Raymond, pointing to the viewscreen. The broken battlecruiser, along with the crippled remnants of four cruisers and a dozen destroyers, were all that was left of Commodore Pearson's Task Force 31.

"Commodore Pearson orders were to hold the system at all costs. Admiral Graves had assured him that the Great Ship would not appear. He was told that it would have to protect the Chameleon home planet in the Cygni star system against the Titans. At least that was President Neumann's thinking after he found out that the Chameleon had only the one Great Ship left."

"The United Planets has been in negotiation with the aliens for over a year," said Gallant. "Was there no progress?"

There was anguish in Raymond's voice. "None. And the Chameleon were angry." He paused, dropping his gaze. "The governor told them to shove off, no deal was possible. After that ultimatum, things turned ugly."

Gallant frowned. "Take your time and start from the beginning."

Raymond's words were clipped. "Task Force 31 had one carrier, four battlecruisers, and two cruiser-destroyer squadrons between planets Charlie and Bravo when the Great Ship appeared. They demanded that the United Planets evacuate the star system. Well, you know Pearson, no way that was happening. He sounded battle stations and ordered his ships to disperse to present a minimal target for the Chameleons."

When Raymond hesitated, Gallant prompted, "What happened next?"

"The action was a disaster—a complete shock. The Chameleon looked at the dispersion as a threat and warned him to stand-down, withdraw, or surrender. After a few minutes, they fired."

He cast his eyes down.

"The single blast was so devastating that it destroyed nearly all our ships. The blinding light and searing heat crippled my *Dauntless* and disintegrated most of the task force. The crippled remainders launched escape pods and waited for a follow-up salvo that, mercifully, never came. We hobbled out of the way. I sent a message to the governor on Charlie." Raymond swallowed hard and furrowed his brow. "The governor's response was to call it 'an unfortunate turn of events.'"

"I learned later that the Chameleon had threatened to make peace with the Titans if we didn't yield the system. They must have since it gave them the freedom of action to leave their home world unprotected and deal with us." He handed Gallant a flash drive. "This contains a plot of the action and the recordings of the communications between our ships and the governor. I've stuck my neck out to get this information on the record. You should collect and check the wreckage along with my observations."

"I understand. Some powerful men in the admiralty will be worried. I will describe the action in a detailed report to be sent to Earth," said Gallant. He worried about how to keep Task Force 34 from suffering the same fate as their predecessor.

CHAPTER 2

Speak Softly

The governor's mansion was nestled on the outskirts of the capital city of the third planet of the Ross star system. More of a rugged concrete bunker than an opulent home, it was designed to withstand Charlie's brutal weather conditions, a planet of rough mountainous terrain blanketed by a thin, volatile atmosphere of noxious gases. A constant stream of sandstorms weathered the building's exterior. The storm's unrelenting howl seeped through the insulated walls until it was no more than an insipid whisper.

From the moment his shuttle landed near the governor's residence, Henry Gallant was on a planet where everything about him, from his heritage to his mission, made him unwelcome. Only the chill night air wrapped around him in greeting. Jagged shards of frost bloomed and crept along the shuttle portals. Foggy wisps of vapor rose off the ground. Winter was impatient to burst forth.

Gallant was met by a bulky man with black

hair and lackluster complexion who ushered him into a hermetically sealed tracked vehicle.

"Are you the captain?" he asked.

"Yes. Captain Henry Gallant of the *Constellation*, commanding Task Force 34. And you are?"

"Cornelius Keyes, the chief of staff to our esteemed governor, Helmut Stein." He hesitated a moment as if weighing his duty to venerate his superior. He added, "He is also vice president of the NNR mining corporation in this system."

Keyes was dressed in a well-tailored black suit with a white shirt and a gold-embroidered waistcoat. His face was a pale open space full of eagerness to please.

Gallant assessed him as a generic sycophant with a perennial bowed head. He asked, "NNR has a presence in this star system? Since when?"

The man's suspicion arose that the captain might be less than an enthusiastic supporter, and his eagerness turned to concern. His nostrils flared like a hound on the scent of prey.

"Since the discovery of massive deposits of essential minerals last year," replied Keyes. "Oh, it's been quite a rich investment for President Gerome Neumann; it has made him the richest man alive. The governor was handpicked by the president to develop the discovery. Everything was going well until this unfortunate event."

Where Gallant was inclined to follow the truth wherever it led, he could tell that Keyes had no room for those who wandered off the prescribed path

—or told tales out of school. Keyes was a loyalist to power.

"You were expected a week ago," said the hulking man. "If you had arrived earlier, maybe things would have been different." His eyes bulged as if he wanted to say more but didn't dare. He yelled at the shuttle driver, "Hurry! We mustn't keep the governor waiting."

They reached the governor's mansion and passed by two guards standing at the gate. Outside the building, the portal was surrounded by bleak rust-colored soil and boulders across the landscape. They were ushered into the governor's office suite.

Governor Helmut Stein was a small crusty man with rigid features. He had a wispy mustache, black hair, and eyes that glistened like black beetles. His lavish dress added to his image as soon-to-be-trillionaire. Of course, that depended on his shares in the Ross Division of the NNR Mining Corporation becoming vested.

"It's about time," growled Stein. "I don't like to be kept waiting."

"We came as quickly as possible, Governor," said Keyes, averting his eyes and bowing his head. "This is the captain."

Gallant stepping forward and said, "Captain Henry Gallant of the *Constellation*."

Gallant recognized the judgmental stare the governor shot at him. He spent a moment reflecting on how he should deal with a man who considered him as a vague curiosity to be treated as a servile attendant. Gallant was always uncomfortable with unscrupulous powerful men. He couldn't comprehend their lack of empathy or integrity. He couldn't find common ground to reconcile their differences without finding drama. In some naïve corner of his heart, he hoped that the governor would behave responsibly, despite his financial conflict of interest.

"Captain, you will make immediate preparations to evacuate my staff and me to Earth along with a massive convoy containing as many tons of the extracted minerals as possible."

Gallant shook his head. "Governor, my first order of business is to disembark the wounded survivors of Task Force 31 to your hospital's rejuvenation chambers. They need extensive medical care."

"Make your needs known to my chief of staff," said Stein indicating Keyes with a hand wave. "He will arrange everything."

Gallant had met enough empty promises in his career to know one when he heard it. Still, he said, "I'll need a dozen shuttles to dock with my ships and transfer the wounded to the planet's hospital, as well as, medical supplies."

Keyes took Gallant's list the supplies. "I'll arrange for the medical staff to be at your disposal." He yapped at Stein's heels like a dog begging for a treat, and then he grinned at Gallant in a forced, toothily way of subservience. "Yes, Captain. I'll arrange everything immediately."

"Now Captain, that we've dispensed with these distractions," the governor said, "you will prepare to evacuate my staff and me to Earth. You have to protect our mineral convoys from that damnable Chameleon ship."

Gallant was bewildered by the governor's judgment of the situation. Could he be completely self-absorbed, or was there a reason behind his decision? He had to work with him regardless.

"I gave you an order."

"No, Governor. You do not have authority over the operational command of my task force. This is a military situation, not a civilian one. My orders were to protect this star system from the threat of the Titans. Now that has extended to the Chameleon."

Gallant watched Stein's face contort as he reassessed the situation. Stein was pondering the risk of remaining in the Ross system as opposed to fleeing back to Earth. Of course, there was also the matter of Neumann's reaction to abandoning his personal mining interests to the enemy.

Stein stroked his chin. "Yet, how will you protect this star system after seeing the destruction of your predecessor?"

"I will protect this system," said Gallant firmly, "because it's my duty." Part of being a good subordinate was keeping your mouth shut about certain things. He watched the governor with growing suspicion.

"I read your extensive personnel file. I am aware of your erratic record and your lack of genetic engineering. I am concerned that it will become a problem," said Stein. He adhered to the genetic engineering protocol of the Neumann administration. He enforced it at Ross. He was mired in the usual mindset of wealthy men who would refer to the possibility of losses with a flick of a finger as if it would sully his reputation.

"Genetic engineering," Stein smugly added, "is for the good of the people."

"All the people?" asked Gallant.

"The ones that count."

Gallant said, "Everyone counts, or no one counts."

Stein stared for a moment and then asked, "How will you fight an invisible enemy? One that is impervious to your weapons and can perform a volcanic blast to destroy your entire task force?"

"I will think on it and find a way. But we are here, and here we will stay," said Gallant, determined to stand fast and fight. Everything about him was fixed on that point. It was a lonely decision, but he was confident that he could find a way to defeat the Great Ship.

"It's risky," said the governor. "Do you believe you can protect this system and the mining extracting, shipping, and processing operations?" Stein looked as if he had started a sentence that Gallant should be able to finish.

There would be a ticking clock waiting for him to fail. They could hold their breathe, but he accepted risk and was prepared to face the enemy. He could already visualize how it might unfold, but its conclusion remained hazy. He immediately began thinking up new plans, but his whole strategy needed revision.

"Though the Great Ship is powerful," he said, "it is only one ship, and it has many commitments. If the Chameleon's home were threatened, the Great Ship would have to leave. Nevertheless, we will prepare, and we will fight wherever and whenever it chooses to appear."

The governor was crafty and greedy. Abandoning the system would deprive him of his money. Gallant guessed that he would be greedy enough to take the gamble.

"The situation is grave and uncertain," said Gallant. "They haven't made any attempt to land troops or drive us off, so the Great Ship may have gone back to her home by now. We will find the enemy and take the initiative. We will force the enemy to react to us. After all, war is ultimately a clash of wills."

"Is your will strong enough?" asked Stein. "The future of this world is now in your hands."

Gallant let a moment pass while he knitted his brow. Then, pressing his lips together, he said, "I must return to my ship and make preparations."

When Gallant reached the *Constellation*, he ordered, "Have Midshipman Daniel Logan report to my cabin."

The OOD replied, "Aye aye, sir."

A few minutes later, there was a rap on his

door.

"Enter."

"Midshipman Logan, reporting as ordered, sir," came a cheery voice.

"Logan, I've got a mission for you. Task Force 34 will remain in this system and face the Great Ship. But if we are to survive, I will need your help to fashion solutions to offset technology advantages the aliens have."

Logan's eyes popped out.

"The excellent work you've done to analyze the Chameleon artifacts and communications were essential in our encounter with the Titan fleet last year. By mimicking the Great Ship, we were able to mislead Admiral Zzey into sending his starfighters off on a wild goose chase while we struck a blow."

"Thank you, sir. I did my best."

"The computer simulations you ran when we attacked the Titan home world, Gliese-Beta, was outstanding as well."

Logan beamed even though he didn't know where this would lead. He was delighted that the captain was satisfied with his efforts.

"Your AI computer skills, as well as your knowledge of the Chameleon, makes you perfect to undertake a vital project I have in mind. This project will require a great deal of ingenuity and perseverance. It will take a considerable effort, and you will be operating independently from the *Constellation* for a good part of that. At some point, I expect it will turn dangerous."

Gallant examined Logan's face, but it showed no reservation, only resolve.

"I will trust you to know when to take a necessary risk and when to back away for the greater good of the mission."

Logan nodded eagerly.

"The Great Ship destroyed Task Force 31 because it had the stealth capability to approach it unawares. Close enough so that the ships couldn't disperse and offer a more difficult target. Then they used their second great technological advantage to blast the task force with one enormous super-laser burst."

Gallant paused before adding, "That's a big stick."

"Yes, sir."

"We're going to need our big stick to penetrate their powerful defensive shield."

Logan furrowed his brow.

"Those three technological challenges—stealth, super-laser, and protective shield—make the Great Ship a deadly enemy. One we will have to face if we remain in the Ross system."

"Yes, sir."

"You are to hunt down every clue in existence about those three riddles and discovering a way to neutralize them."

"Sir, I don't ... I mean how am I going to ..."

"It seems daunting, but I believe you will succeed. I am authorizing you to act independently. And I am giving you three assets to help you accomplish this mission. First, you will contact a forensic xenoarchaeologist named Kate Mahoney at the Bletchley Center on Charlie. She's a civilian analyst who works for SIA. Like you, she has been studying the Chameleon for over a year and is the leading expert in this system. You'll find her invaluable to ferret out the clues necessary to solve the three puzzles."

Gallant handed Logan a file folder with Mahoney's name on the tab. Logan took a quick look. She worked inside the SAI bunker on Charlie on a cipher team to decode secret enemy communications.

"Second, she has access to an AI quantum supercomputer. It's a hundred times more powerful than the *Constellation's* computer. It will be invaluable in running your simulations and analytic studies. Third, I am placing the *Warrior* at your disposal to travel secretly to wherever necessary to acquire clues and artifacts. Captain Roberts will be a helpful sounding board if you need advice, while the *Constellation* is out of range."

Gallant took a deep breath. "This will not be easy or quick, but the task force's survival will depend on your ability to solve the three puzzles. If possible, solve the stealth puzzle first. That will allow me to keep tabs on the Great Ship while other events unfold."

"I worked with several CIC techs before who were helpful with Chameleon's ship," said Logan. "I could use them."

"I'll assign them to your team to help sort through the SIA and military intelligence that the agencies have collected. So far, they haven't had much luck finding the Chameleon secrets. It's going to be up to you and your team to uncover the 'magic' behind the stealth, laser, and shield technologies."

Logan stood tall.

"Go to Charlie and contact Kate Mahoney. Her expertise and the quantum supercomputer will be the 'secret sauce' you will need to crack this."

"Aye aye, sir."

CHAPTER 3

Kate Mahoney

Her life was not as nice as it once was, and Kate had been depressed lately, well, not just lately. She was mostly depressed forever. Depression was a common side-effect of loss and uncertainty, and her existence had become bewildering since her mother's death. How different her life might have been with her mother to guide and protect her.

Kate focused her attention on the faded crinkled photo that had long ago lost its luster and resilience, yet it was more precious to her than gold. It was the only original image she had of her mother. She burned the picture into her mind. At the time the photo was taken, her mother was a twenty-year-old brunette with an athletic figure. She was wearing a bathing suit sitting on a blanket, leaning back on her elbows with her legs extended, flashing a vivacious smile. Kate imagined all the good things in her mother's life that could have coaxed that expression from her. When she looked into her eyes, she saw the years they might have shared. Her finger traced her mother's figure and caressed her face. It was the only tactile connection left. She wondered if her mother had been as afraid to face each day as she was. Though she knew almost nothing of her mother's life, she imagined her as a kind and giving soul.

They say that there is no greater grief than that of a mother who has lost her child, but Kate could tell them from personal experience that a child who loses her mother suffers equally, even after years have passed.

She tucked the photo back into her jacket pocket and returned to her work, hoping to escape the emotions welling up in her.

She examined an ancient Chameleon artifact under a microscope. Except for the scope illumination, the top-secret Bletchley Circle laboratory was dark.

Her concentration was broken by a figure dressed in overalls bursting through the door. His arms were full of bulky boxes that looked as if they would topple into a great heap at any moment.

Surprised out of her reverie, she reflexively jumped a little, embarrassed at being caught alone in the dark.

"Who the hell are *you*?" she demanded.

The young man stared at her blankly for a second, squinting against the darkness.

She swiped on the lights and marched toward him, her heels clicking on the tile floor. "Cat got your tongue? Speak up."

The young man looked distressed as she

halted mere inches from his face and examined him with a critical eye. She thought he was about her age and...*hmmm...he's rather cute.*

"I'm Logan," he said, and then he smiled, bowed his head, and added, "At your service,"

She frowned. "This is a restricted area. What are you doing here?"

He looked about as if trying to decide how he could unload his burden of boxes. "I'm afraid I got turned around in that last corridor. I'm trying to hook up with a forensic xenoarchaeologist, Kate Mahoney."

He tilted his head to gain a better viewing angle from behind his stack of boxes before asking, "Is that you?"

Kate was a tall, slender, twenty-year-old math prodigy. Her tomboy ponytail was often noticed streaking through the halls as she sprinted from one laboratory to another. She furrowed her brows that had spent much of their lifetime pinched together, illustrating her penchant for getting lost in thought.

"I'm Kate Mahoney, but I wasn't expecting anyone. Show me your badge."

"Things are moving pretty quick. I just got my clearance, and my paperwork hasn't been passed through channels, but it should be online." He started to maneuver his load of boxes onto the tabletop.

"Careful! You'll knock over my microscope."

She checked her computer. After a few keystrokes, she read out loud from the access list, "Midshipman Daniel Logan of the *Constellation*? Captain

Gallant sent you?"

Logan nodded. He eased his boxes onto the table and then turned to face her.

She frowned. "To do what exactly?"

Logan said, "There should be detailed orders in your in-basket."

She opened an email attachment and quickly read through the instructions. "To solve problems in dealing with the crisis of the Great Ship in this star system," she read. "How are we supposed to do that?"

"There are several technology puzzles about the Great Ship that Captain Gallant hopes we can solve to stop the threat."

"Why me? I don't know anything about fighting space battles."

"You're a leading expert on the Chameleon. Evaluating key aspects of their technology could be essential to countering it."

"Why you? You look kind of... pardon me... young and an *amateur*." She saw him as a baby officer just out of the Academy from his age and eagerness.

Logan grimaced, "*Amateur*? That's uncalled for. I'm an expert at running AI simulations."

"AI simulations?"

"Yeah."

"Well, that might actually be useful. All my Chameleon data is stored on a quantum supercomputer that runs in a virtual world."

"A virtual world simulation of the Great Ship? Really? That would be fun to explore."

She found his geeky demeanor and lack of

filter somewhat appealing.

She said, "It's not for fun. It's a serious tool for exploring the Chameleon systems and technology. I've devoted a year to install complex software to mimic the physics equations guiding the technology. At least, as best as I could extrapolate from the data collected from observations of the Great Ship's operations."

"I don't doubt that you've done a wonderful job. I can think of a dozen ways we can use it to explore solutions to the puzzles Captain Gallant has given us."

"What puzzles?"

Logan said, "Let me start at the beginning. The Titan destroyed all the other Great Ships over the last century. They found that once the Chameleon fired their super-laser, they remained weak long enough for the Titans to launch suicide attacks that destroyed the Great Ships. Now we face this last monster in our system. Captain Gallant wants an expert team to find a way to destroy it without having to sacrifice our fleet."

"Team?"

"Well, for now, it's you, me, and whatever tech support we can scrounge up."

"I see," she said, softly. Something shifted in her eyes, like a drawbridge falling open. "You're right. My AI quantum supercomputer can run simulations of the Great Ship that could be helpful. Follow me to the basement without disturbing the others," she said in a conspiratorial hush.

Logan said, "Thanks."

"This'll give me a chance to show off my work."

Logan beamed. "Show me everything."

She led him past the security checkpoint in the middle of the ground floor. Taking the staircase to the basement, they followed a central corridor all the way to the back corner of the building. All the while, they listened to the wind howling outside the bunker. The secluded computer room housed the AI quantum supercomputer. It covered the entire back wall from floor to ceiling. A server farm covered the opposite wall.

Logan's eyes grew wide. He said, "Ever since quantum computers achieve supremacy over ordinary computers, I've wanted to play with one. Now I've got a super one."

Kate knitted her brow at the hint of Logan's possessiveness. She said, "My AI uses neural net software running on a computer. Unlike the human neurons, neural nets are encoded in bits on hard disks. While neural nets have mere thousands of neurons, the human brain has 100 billion."

Her keycard gave them access to the control room where they were bathed by the soft glow of computer screens. She spent a few minutes explaining the operation and then showed him a few simple examples.

She said, "Let's get one thing straight. I'm good at what I do, and I usually work alone. I'm willing to follow Captain Gallant's orders and include you. But if you slow me down, I'm cutting you loose."

Logan turned beet red. "Look, I'm good at what I do, too. In fact, I'm going to beat you at solving every one of these puzzles."

Kate laughed, "I don't think so, but I like competition. You're on!"

She showed him how to access the QC simulation with a new state-of-the-art immersive rig. "Here, put on this gear, and we can take a virtual tour of the Great Ship and my personal library of data."

After pulling on the hand and head rig, Logan waited while Kate turned on the immersive environment. His view of the room shrank into a thumbnail in the corner of his peripheral vision, allowing him to exist in the virtual reality world. The world was divided into sections of knowledge databases and environments. His avatar appeared at the gallery entrance, and his reflection in the glass showed it looked like himself.

After a minute, Kate's avatar joined his in the central gallery. Kate's avatar looked exactly like her as well.

She waved her hand. "We can wade through every piece of Chameleon data available within this repository and give commands to analyze whatever we want. We can take part in the simulations we want to explore. Pretty neat, huh?"

"Yeah! I'll say. I may never want to leave this place. It's great."

She illustrated the versatility of the machine to solve forensic archaeology tasks. By manipulating her fingers, she stretched the Great Ship model. It gave them access to any corner of the gigantic ship, and she strolled through its corridors and showed Logan various items. She could rotate the model and stretch the model at will, and it was clear the value of exploring all the Chameleons artifacts through this method.

"Impressive," said Logan.

After an hour of demos and examples, they exited the virtual world and sat together at the center table in the laboratory to drink coffee and make plans. Logan began unpacking the boxes of material he had brought. It had lots of data on Chameleon, and they scanned the information into the computer.

He said, "I've got lots of data that we can use to upgrade the physics models you used to illustrate the Chameleon technology. I've got data from Captain McCall and the SAI's espionage on the Great Ship when she was at Cygni. She had unearthed significant scientific databases relating to key Chameleon technology. We can use it to unearth the secrets behind their super-lasers, stealth capabilities, and shield technologies."

"I don't know. The Chameleon are awfully smart."

"I'm smart too," said Logan. "And we probably got ninety-nine percent of the data we need."

"It's always that last one percent that kills you."

CHAPTER 4

Gold Braid

The *Constellation's* ready room was rapidly filling with captains. The task force leaders took seats on the starboard side. Captains Hernandez of the *Invincible* and Captain Jackson of the *Courageous* took their place in the first row. Captains of the cruisers, destroyers, and support ships filled in behind them. The opposite side of the cavernous room filled with the civilian captains of tankers, cargo ships, transports, and space tugs. Several NNR mining managers found places in the first row. It was a gathering of glittering gold braid that featured furtive looks firing between the two spaceship commands.

Gallant stood at the podium, facing the dubious military and civilian audiences. All the faces around the room reflected uncertainty and impatience.

"Officers and leaders of the Ross star system, welcome!" announced Gallant in a booming voice.

His eyes roamed the room. "The traumatic loss of Task Force 31 has caused understandable alarm. But I am confident that, if we band together, we can continue to send essential materials to Earth."

There was an uncomfortable stir throughout the room, and he distinctly heard the alien names called out, "Titans" and "Chameleon."

He raised his hands to quiet the audience. "Our central problem is that ore must be mined on the outer planets and transported to Charlie for processing before it can be shipped to Earth. And yes, the alien threat is daunting. Titan cruiser-destroyer squadrons are raiding throughout the system. And we have no idea where the Great Ship is or if it will coordinate with the Titans."

The NNR manager, Grover Miller, whose sour face matched his mood, stood. A neatly trimmed beard framed his self-satisfied smirk. He said, "Captain Gallant, our material is essential for the survival United Planets. We expect you to protect us."

Gallant guessed that many of the civilians were sincere in their desire to help the war effort. But was the NNR manager wasn't more interested in the wealth his stock options would earn.

"The presence of the Titan raiders makes it necessary for our transport to travel in convoys with adequate escorts," said Miller. "However, the convoys will be juicy targets for the Chameleon and their Great Ship's super-laser."

Every head in the room nodded, and every eye searched Gallant for a way out of the dilemma.

Miller said, "We can't just start and stop operations on a planet or during transport. Our operations are complex and time-sensitive. Much of it is robotically controlled, and delays cause ripple effects throughout our organization. For example, mining operations require drilling, blasting, and transporting a variety of materials. That doesn't even address the need to crush, grind, and process them for production. We don't have enough equipment operators, so we use robotic mining equipment to dig shafts using smart drills that can sense the type of material. Sensors provide data for remote control operations that reduce human labor. But those devices need AI control. Also, we incorporate remote automation of our big moving machinery. We have to load and unload huge space cargo vessels; each is as large as the *Constellation*."

"I understand," said Gallant. "It is the cargo vessels that present the greatest problem. They are unmanned, unpowered hulks filled with millions of tons of ore. You join many of them together in a tandem arrangement pulled by strong cables attached to a super space tug. You call it a space train, an efficient use of men and machine but one that is extraordinarily hard to maneuver. A space train requires extraordinary navigation skills because of the incredible inertia. You can't maneuver or stop without elaborate planning."

Captain Wells, a rather bulky man with balding gray hair, was the space tug consortium's leader. He said, "That's right. One tug can pull dozens of cargo containers behind it. It's very efficient, and a convoy can consist of many trains. But each space train would be forty or fifty kilometers long. A layer of ten columns of space trains could fly side by side. Then another layer of ten space trains would fly above and another below. A convoy of thirty space trains in three layers of ten would include three hundred cargo container vessels. That convoy would form a cube fifty kilometer on a side. How can you provide escort coverage around 125,000 cubic kilometers of space?"

"Yes. That makes them a plumb target," said Captain Daux, tipping back in his chair. He was another space tug captain with influence. Together they were the key leaders that would decide how to allocate the star systems scant manpower and ship resources.

More than one grim face turned pale as a murmur of protest swept the room

Gallant said, "I've divided Task Force 34 into four strike forces. Each is assigned to escort one of four convoys that will travel through the Ross system. They will move fully loaded from the outer planets to Charlie and then return empty to their origin. Special arrangements will be made when a shipment is ready for transport to Earth. No other ships will travel outside of these convoys."

"Captain Gallant," said Wells. "I, for one, regret that we are moving in a rather hasty manner. Based on the danger posed by the Great Ship, it's clear that you need to do more to protect us."

The meeting dragged on for another hour.

Gallant's hands were clenched on the podium. He didn't tap his fingers or twitch a brow. But under the podium, his shoes tapped a beat to the seconds as they dragged on. He was impatient with the undisciplined civilian attitude. His plan was prepared, but the civilians didn't seem receptive. He'd listened to their complaints. His head was buzzed with their disagreeable voices. The longer the discussion went on, the more unbearable it became.

He said, "The final details and adjustments will be worked through my XO, Commander Fletcher. If you have questions or concerns, contact her after this meeting. For now, it is imperative that you understand that this has already been approved by Governor Stein and my task force commanders."

Fletcher rose. Her soothing soprano voice became the center of attention. She said, "I've just sent each of you a digital file detailing the convoy schedule. Each convoy will consist of up to 300 cargo vessels. That's 30 space trains with up to ten cargo vessels each. It will take days of constant acceleration to get each train to 0.1 C, and then they wouldn't be able to change course or speed without great difficulty. So, everything about them must be extensively planned. You will find your ship assignments and requirements on the attached file."

The room erupted into noisy chatter as the civilian captains were scrolling through assignments and orders. They compared routes and schedules.

Fletcher said, "I look forward to working with you to accommodate your suggestions to our mutual needs. The first convoy leaving Alpha will be designated Alpha001. Bravo will be designated Bravo001.

Those leaving Charlie to go to Earth will be designed E001 and so on. I am willing to listen to any of your operational recommendations."

Miller gave a dry cough. "Naturally, the NNR Corporation has its corporate needs, but we are willing to consider your priorities."

"Fine," said Fletcher, a frown spreading across her face.

CHAPTER 5

Puzzled

Once again, Kate was startled when Logan popped up before her lab door in the Bletchley Circle bunker.

"Remember me?" asked Logan, his grin and happy voice was a distinct contrast to her foul mood.

"Huh?" She said, "You're late. You were supposed to start work an hour ago. I hate late people. It's so easy to be on time. All you have to do is be early and early lasts for hours. On-time only lasts a minute. Then you're late."

She gave him a caustic look with furrowed brows and pouty lips.

"It took longer than I thought to gather this last artifact," said Logan, shaking off her admonishment without a care.

"Look," he said, handing the object to her.

Her anger vanished as she was instantly transfixed in curiosity. "Cool," she said as she rotated it in her hands. The ancient tool had markings she copied into her translator. "This is crazy. It's a calibration instrument that tunes the frequency of a laser. This is a great find."

A smile broke out on her face.

Logan asked, "How do you want to start working?"

She asked, "Well, let me ask you about your approach to solving puzzles. For example, how would you solve a simple two-dimensional jigsaw puzzle?"

"Hmmm, . . ., I would start by forming a clear working space and follow a dedicated timetable. Unlike some impatient people, I don't immediately jump into fitting pieces together—the probability of finding matching pieces, right off the bat, is minuscule."

He grinned at his own cleverness, but Kate smirked.

He continued, "I would examine every piece in the puzzle meticulously. That may seem tedious, but it builds familiarity and sets up the following steps. My goal would be to maximize the number of clues and minimize the pool of options. I'm sure that reduces the overall time. Then I would sort pieces by the most easily distinguished features, such as color and pattern, setting aside corners and edges. Next, I would divide the pieces into piles of smaller collections based on their number of tabs and blanks. I start building the rim from a corner or an edge piece. Then I would fit the picture together, piece by piece."

Kate shook her head and sighed, clearly unhappy with his prescriptive approach. "Logical. Typical."

"Thank you. I'd like to think so." Logan threw back his shoulders.

"That wasn't a compliment," Kate screeched. "Typical logic won't work in atypical situations like ours. We must find out how an alien mind thinks. How they went about building this technology."

Logan looked as downcast as a little boy who had his ice cream cone knocked from his hand.

Kate's whole being was animated as she said, "We're not going to solve these puzzles unless we think 'blue-sky' 'out-of-the-box' stuff. Analyzing alien technology is too big a task for a limited prescription of logical steps. It requires ingenious creativity. Negative thoughts and preemptive limitations will kill the kind of innovation we need."

"I don't understand," said Logan, knitting his brow. "What exactly do you propose?"

"Maybe you're a practical type who wants everything to be perfectly logical and explained in detail. You haven't ever found yourself in an unexpected place with a surprising puzzle. Or maybe you think of mysteries as a waste of your time and talent. But I know mysteries can lead to magical places and rewarding experiences."

"Magical places?"

"No." Kate sighed. "Not actual *magic* magic, but a delightfully mysterious discovery."

Logan groaned. "What are you saying?"

"When I was eight, I found a metal box about this big." Kate held her hands out in front of her, ten centimeters apart. "It was made of a smooth material I've never seen before. It had mysterious symbols on it. One mark caught my attention. I swear I recognized it as something profoundly important, yet I couldn't quite place it. I imagined this wasn't an ordinary run-of-the-mill box, but one with precious riches inside. That made me excited and curious. I called it my treasure chest. I looked everywhere for a key, but there was none. I tried to break open the lock. It wouldn't budge. I carried it to my room and looked for something to pry it open with."

"So?"

"A key is a powerful thing. When you have one, it opens the door to a treasure. When you can't find a key, you are left outside in frustration."

Animated, Logan asked, "What was in the box?"

She shook her head. "You don't know a thing about me. You could imagine me sitting at some small wooden desk in my bedroom with that chest propped up against the wall. As I take a knife and twist the chest's lock, a breeze blows in from the open window and tickles the back of my neck. Then, I find something wonderful and magical inside that chest."

A baffled look came over Logan's face. "So? Did that actually happen?"

"You look at me," said Kate, "and see my pale skin and soft hair, but you know nothing of my past. I suppose you could speculate about me based on my background and expertise. But you don't know what it meant to me to solve the puzzle of that treasure chest. There could be a thousand stories about that chest. Who had it? Who used it? What did it contain before I found it?"

Logan stared into Kate's intense eyes.

She said, "Maybe I was destined to find it. Or it was destined never to be found, and I disturbed a profound truth. The dividing point between real and imagined, you and me, things of this world or another world, that's where imagination lives. You need imagination to overcome unusual challenges and to solve inscrutable puzzles."

Logan crossed his arms and growled, "Are you going to tell me what was in the chest."

"Just what I expected, straight to the point, no finesse at all." She stood up and placed her hands akimbo. "No, Daniel, I'm not! At least not now. You haven't earned the right."

"I solve puzzles," said a defiant Logan. "I'll leave magical mysteries to you."

"Okay, smart guy, make sense of this trivial literary puzzle . . ." Kate typed a passage into his tablet, "That that is is that that is not is not is that it it is it is what it is."

"That's nonsensical gobbledygook," said Logan, shoving the tablet back at her.

"It seems that way at first glance from a macro point of view, but if you examine the detail, and use your imagination, you could find the solution," she laughed. "It's perfectly sensible with the proper punctuation. Here, look."

She retyped the passage.

That that is, is.
That, that is not, is not.
Is that it?
It is.
It is what it is.

"Am I to learn your technique of solving puzzles from that?"

"I could tell from the moment we met that you were a 'big picture' kind of guy. You like to examine the macroscopic ideas to understand how something works. From that, you dig down into the component parts of what the whole is made of."

"I suppose you're right," said Logan. "I find that the global view is the easiest way to understand a complex system. Isn't that the way you solve a puzzle?"

Kate smirked. "No. I'm just the opposite. The brain is capable of a lot of parallel processing, and I like to look at puzzles as multifaceted and attack the detail parts in parallel."

"You start with the details?"

She squinted as if focusing her mind. "Not just the details. I hunt out the smallest, most essential unique element from which everything else must be derived. If there is a small unique item, then it must be the critical ingredient that makes everything else work? Once you establish its exclusive ability, you can extrapolate the construction of the entire apparatus. For example, if you understand how a transistor works, you can understand how to build a computer chip."

"I guess that's valid," he said reluctantly. "But I'm concerned that we are going to be at odds working together."

"Not at all," said Kate. "Every day, you make choices, choices from hope, and choices of fear. Sometimes, they make your life better, sometimes, not. I wake up every day with a desire to pursue my passion, finding patterns, solving puzzles. Math is full of hidden secrets that expose the world through symmetry and patterns."

Logan nodded.

She continued, "We should work to solve these puzzles using our natural talents. With you working from above and me working from below, we will arrive at an elegant solution in the middle. It's likely that our efforts will fit together. That alone will tell us that we have found the correct solution."

"I like that. Let's get started."

She explained the quantum computer's advantage. "Binary computers require data bits encoded into zeros or ones. Quantum computer uses quantum bits, which allow superpositions of states. Consider quantum bits on a classical three-bit register. If the exact state is not known, it can be described as a probability distribution over the eight different three-bit strings: 000, 001, etc. If there is no uncertainty, it is exactly one state with probability one. However, for our probabilistic computer, there is a possibility associated with each different state."

Logan said, "That's what allows for the speed

and flexibility of the quantum computer?"

"Yes."

The pair donned their immersive VR suits and entered the Great Ship virtual world.

"We've spent all our time in this simulation exploring ideas about the people and the operations."

"I've tried to speculate on the relationship to some of the older artifacts to the Great Ship simulation."

Kate said, "For the past year, I've been devoted to going through the SAI spy drone data to build my virtual Great Ship world. I've made notes on the missing sections that the spy drone couldn't penetrate. I've studied every translated word to get insight into the technology's operation. The more I've learned, the more curious I got."

Logan said, "Let's unpack the data I brought and get busy exploring. We have to map out what we know and what we need to find out."

"Why does this feel like the first day of school?" asked Kate.

"Huh, maybe. Anyway, let's get started."

The rest of the day passed quietly in deep concentration, resolving their own special problems. Then they got together to brainstorm. Logan watched the recordings of the military action when the Great Ship fought in the Gliese star system. It fired its super-laser and used stealth technology to leave the system. There were also clues about its shield strength.

After they completed several hours of exploration in the VR, they exited the immersive world.

"It's a bit jolting transitioning between virtual and real," Kate said.

Logan said, "Yeah. I think I'm done for today."

A rustling howl cut into their conversation.

"Hear that?" asked Kate.

"Are you okay? You seem really far away."

"It sounds like whispering," she said, tensing her shoulders.

"Are you messing with me?"

CHAPTER 6

Convoy

The doubts and concerns which intruded into Gallant's sleep vanished with the dawn. He felt renewed strength running through his veins as he began his morning ritual. His mind teemed with plans with each step on his tour through the ship. He devised a convoy system with adequate escorts and issued the execution orders within hours.

A few days later, Gallant's heart leaped when he finally got the first convoy moving with his strike force 34.4.1 as escort. In the first hour of the morning watch, the viewscreen showed the Ross star as a bright dot in the center of the monitor. The formation of space trains and escorts looked like crisscrossing streets in a busy downtown city. Compared to the enormity of space, the convoy was but a speck, as the ships proceeded like an arrow pointed at planet Charlie. A ring of asteroids formed a curtain in their path.

The convoy's first day was a ragged confused affair as the civilians struggled to keep on station. They strayed from Gallant's disciplined orders, but slowly they were meeting his demands. There was anger and resentment. The civilians weren't happy about the risk they were taking with the Great Ship on the loose.

Despite the poor course keeping of the civilian vessels, the irregular assembly made its way forward. Even if the civilian ships' professionalism had matched the military, the aged vessels had creaks and groans that spoiled their performance. The crew's hands turned the valves and pressed the switches, and human reactions were slow, whether careless or unskilled. It was easy enough for someone to select the wrong button or the wrong wheel to turn. The crews were trained for normal operations. The question was, how prepared were they if they had to react to an emergency?

The *Constellation* was on full alert, but that was less than comforting since the enemy was capable of stealth and maneuver. The task force formed a self-reinforcing spherical formation for protection.

On the surface, the limited area this force enclosed bore many ships and large crews. Solar flares rolled across space and crashed against the ships, each without noticeable effect. The transports, cargo ships, and ore freighters were a mix of new and old. Yet they drove on, animated by the will for the task force commander.

There were twenty thousand people in the convoy. The property was worth uncountable billions. The raw material was on its way to being turned into a critical mineral that would be shipped to Earth. It would help the war effort, as well as line the pockets of President Neumann.

For several days, Gallant and Fletcher worked to reorganize the schedule to improve the efficiency of the shipments.

"Task force units are reporting in compliance to your orders, sir," reported the OOD.

"Very well," said Gallant.

"All except the *Star Rover*. She has a problem."

"That's Captain Wells isn't it?"

"Yes, sir."

"Keep your eye on that space train. At least, our convoy is underway. The second convoy is coming together at Bravo."

"Aye aye, sir," said Fletcher. "There are tonnage updates available for your review about the processing of minerals at Charlie."

After reviewing the data, Gallant said, "This is serious. The production schedule has completely broken down. We must get things rolling to meet the shipping dates for Earth."

"Aye aye, sir."

He spent several hours with the XO revising schedules in hopes of correcting the problems. But millions of kilometers ahead of them, the men and women of Charlie awaited their arrival. And the convoy might have to face burning hot lasers along the way. There were cultures worth fighting for and values worth protecting, but that fact didn't reduce the danger.

Gallant spent a moment reflecting on his career in his cabin. Of the ten years that had passed since he had left the academy, almost all had been spent in space and at war. His first ship was the interplanetary battlecruiser *Repulse*. He had served aboard the first FTL ship, the *Intrepid*, on its maiden voyage to Elysium. Soon afterward, he had been given command of his first ship, the *Warrior*. Each challenge offered broader experience. But since taking over the *Constellation*, he faced the extra burden of commanding a task force with far more ships and lives at stake than ever.

A call cut into his recollections.

"Captain to the bridge! Captain to the bridge!" blared the intercom.

The OOD's voice carried an urgency that drove Gallant from his day cabin to the bridge in the record time of twelve seconds. He scanned the viewport and instrument panel before turning to face the OOD, Lieutenant Carlson. Gallant was pleased to be working with such a resourceful, diligent young man, one who displayed a keen, alert mind.

Gallant glanced at Carlson, and the OOD said, "The *Warrior* reported a possible distant contact, sir."

"Possible contact? Why the uncertainty?"

"The *Warrior* has identified a space distortion field ahead of the convoy that could be manmade. Its characteristics are unique and troubling. They speculated that it might be an aberration due to fluctuations in a massive stealth field. We haven't detected it aboard the *Constellation*, but looking at the data, the *Warrior* has indicated it could be a massive object."

"How massive?" Gallant asked the CIC officer, William Jacobs, who was considered a marginal officer.

"It's too early to know, sir," Jacobs replied, "but possibly many kilometers."

"Your suspicion is that the Great Ship could be nearby, and its stealth shield may be faulty?"

"Ah . . . well, sir . . ." Jacobs hemmed. "It's a possibility." The CIC officer's voice betrayed his discomfort in reporting such flimsy information to his commanding officer.

"Sir," the communication officer said, "the *Warrior* requests permission to break formation and investigate the distortion."

"Permission to investigate granted,"

Gallant glanced at the task force's position on the monitor and noted the lax formation of several civilian ships.

How can AI computers be so far off course? What inattention to detail could cause such errors?

He hesitated as he considered several possibilities. The words of warning represented a problem of vast complexity. Could the anomaly be a natural phenomenon? A stealth system failure? It was conceivable this was an accidental distortion caused by the Great Ship that it might not yet be aware of. If so, sending the *Warrior* to investigate could tip off the enemy. Gallant dismissed that thought. Any failure significant enough to produce such an anomaly would be apparent to the Great Ship immediately.

Gallant said. "This must be a Titan raider with

strong stealth capabilities. We occasionally get a whiff of them, but they're quick to slip away. We have to deal with that contingency while we stay vigilant against the possibility of the Great Ship reappearing."

Gallant considered a score of options to deal with what could develop into a complex and dangerous situation. He was not well-positioned to confront the Great Ship and ensure the safety of the convoy. Should he wait for more information or act quickly? He ran the formation position in his mind and tried to determine if he should change formation or just reposition the outer ships. He could expect poor performance from the civilian convoy, and that might create confusion, a situation he couldn't afford.

On the other hand, he had to maximize his security. Gallant scanned the information screen for ideas. The distortion was dead ahead. It remained ominous and unlikely to be random. Only Task Force 34.4 was available to cover the convoy while the other three strike forces were dispersed around the star system. He could contact one of the other task force units, but the nearest was days away. He could warn the planets, but that would do no good. If the distortion was the Great Ship, was it preparing to attack, or was it merely assessing the situation? There had been no recent sightings. Could the distortion be a Titan ship? Several political factors played in his mind. He could dismiss Stein's reaction to a reappearance of the Great Ship. What were his crew and task force members thinking of him now? Did they have faith in him? Would he be too rash? Too cautious? Would they second guess his every action?

He watched as the tracking vector showed the *Warrior* heading toward the shimmering distortion. He glanced at the clock. It had been less than one minute since he had reached the bridge. It was time to act, so he ordered several destroyers to move forward and deployed ships and starfighters.

"Launch the standby Hawkeye," he ordered.

A few minutes later, the Hawkeye joined the *Warrior* in the investigation.

"Sir," the communication officer interjected, "we are getting a lot of query traffic from the convoy. They want to know if there is immediate danger."

"Send: all ships to remain alert; no need for alarm," Gallant responded. He continued to track the *Warrior* and the Hawkeye's progress as they worked their way to the target area.

Gallant ordered, "Officer of the deck, order task force to change course to zero three zero, mark two, ahead standard."

It was a trifling alteration, but it would make a huge difference over time. He listened as the OOD relayed his order and the convoy captains responded.

Finally, the OOD ordered, "Execute!"

The convoy began to alter course. The huge fifty-kilometer cube of space tugs straining to pull cargo containers after the minor change in direction.

As Gallant watched the formation change on his monitor, he was taken aback when the vector icon of one of the space tugs blinked but failed to turn.

That tug's space train was plowing straight ahead, threatening to cause more collisions than he could contemplate.

He yelled, "Officer-of-the-deck, send an urgent kick-in-the-butt to space tug G034F. Tell Captain Wells to execute the course change, immediately!"

The OOD opened the communication channel and conveyed the order in no uncertain terms. A minute later, the tug began turning.

After several tense minutes, the OOD reported, "Convoy steady on course zero three zero, mark two, ahead standard."

The XO appeared at Gallant's elbow, her face tense. "Should we send the ships to general quarters, sir?" she asked.

He made a mental note of how quickly Fletcher was to sound general quarters. He wavered. Men and women were fatigued and stressed. It wouldn't do to add to their burden until he knew for sure there was an actual problem.

"Not yet."

"Sir," the OOD reported, "the destroyer *Conway* requests permission to join the *Warrior*."

The *Conway* was the point destroyer and her skipper, Parker Schaffer, was keen to get involved.

But leaving the point position would create a gap in the convoy's protection, so he quickly responded, "Permission denied."

He then received a data report from the *Warrior*. CIC ran a simulation against possible natural phenomena that might cause such a distortion, but the results were ambiguous.

Gallant returned to scanning the viewscreen and his parameter readouts. He also ran through the performance and position of the civilian ships. Several were keeping poor formation.

"Sir," the OOD said, "the *Warrior* reports the distortion signal is growing weaker and more dispersed."

"Can't they get a range and bearing?"

"No, sir. It appears to be coming from many different points."

"Keep sweeping the area."

Gallant then ordered the convoy to change course again.

Finally, the OOD reported, "We've lost contact."

"Order the *Warrior* to return to formation," Gallant commanded.

The convoy resumed its course and speed. Every change was a concern because he couldn't depend on the civilian convoy ships. There was always the possibility of confusion and even collision. If one ship failed to execute his orders precisely, the convoy would be unbalanced and thrown into confusion. All he and his crew could do was to remain vigilant and hope for the best.

The target popped up again several hours

later.

"Target bearing zero one zero, mark two." The OOD's voice was calm, alert, and professional.

"Change course to zero one zero, mark two." The helmsman repeated the order and then made the adjustment. A moment later, he reported the new heading.

"CIC, what do you make of the target?"

"Dead ahead, sir, but no clear identification." Jacobs reported from the CIC, "The bearing is changing. Now it's zero two zero."

The range had decreased, and the detection equipment was analyzing at light speed.

Gallant considered launching additional starfighters. Instead, he directed the CSP to the target for a better evaluation.

"We are within missile range now," the CIC reported.

He could open fire, but Gallant was on a collision course with the target. His instincts told him to beware. It could be a Titan ship, so he decided to remain patient.

The solar flares were acting up and may have prompted the unknown skipper to change course. It was imperative to close the distance surreptitiously. The plot showed an intercept course with some cover. It was unlikely the unknown vessel would linger without a specific purpose but discovering its goal would not be easy. It was worthwhile to attempt to re-establish contact. What would her next move be? What was his best countermove? A trivial course change now would mean a significant deviation after a few hours.

"Warn me when we've reached the last known position," Gallant said.

"Aye aye, sir."

A more perceptive man might have noticed the disappointment in the officer's voice. There was a general letdown among the bridge crew after the tense hours of 'hunt and seek.' But if the unknown ship turned up soon, that would immediately change. Captain Gallant ordered a change in speed. The increased vibrations were felt on deck as he issued the command to have the Hawkeye swing through the area once more.

Gallant listened to the Hawkeye's data report with keen interest, but there was no new information. Seconds crept by until he heard, "Contact, sir."

Everyone on the bridge tensed at the news.

"Very well." Gallant held himself steady, hardly breathing, as he awaited the next report.

"Target may be a Titan ship," Carlson reported. "We have its course and speed."

"Match them," Gallant ordered.

Minutes passed.

"Contact lost."

What was this ship—a will-of the-wisp? Gallant wondered.

"We have contact again."

Gallant decided to increase speed and charge down to the point.

"Range decreasing."

They moved closer to the mystery ship, but a minute later, they seemed to be circling each other. Gallant analyzed the tactical situation and found it peculiar.

If it turned out to be Titan raiders, their only option was to fight through them, so Gallant hoped they wouldn't be joined by the Great Ship any time soon. Everyone had to do their jobs to get through this, and one battle at a time would be enough. Gallant returned his attention to finding the best course to penetrate a screen of Titan raiders.

"Change course to zero three zero, mark two," he commanded.

The convoy made the change and slowly wiggled in small adjustments to correct the imperfections in their relative positions. When their rippling dance concluded ten minutes later, Gallant sighed at the computer illustration of the neatly aligned ships. It was the best he could have hoped for.

Carlson stood at Gallant's side, his face intense, but confident. Was the OOD's confidence placed in his own abilities or in his belief that his captain would get them through this—or both. In any event, Gallant wanted to reestablish contact with the unknown ship rather than guess its location.

"Possible distant contact one-nine-five. Range indefinite."

"Incoming missiles! Bearing one-nine-five..."

He didn't finish...

CHAPTER 7

Showman

The *Constellation* escorted the first massive convoy to reach Charlie. The arrival was greeted with much fanfare. The public event was broadcast on all news outlets and celebrated by businesses and an anxious population.

Gallant waited as Helmut Stein exited his shuttle. He watched as the governor strode along the enclosed gangplank to enter the *Constellation*. Stein looked eager to bask in the glow of this success. His face wore an expression of childish delight as he gazed at the row of warships and cargo vessels nuzzled together in orbit over the planet. He turned to the news cameras broadcasting the event to the inhabitants of the planet. He had promised the public that he would provide for their safety, and this photo op was his best endorsement. The theatrical display of military might encourage an enthusiastic response from the public. He waved to the cameras and imagined the cheering crowds. Surrounding him on the platform was a cluster of naval officers. Among them was Commander Fletcher, who agreed to conduct him on a tour of the ship. Gallant was reluctant to participate in the stunt despite understanding its propaganda value.

Stein gave a long and disjointed speech to the cameras, subject to changes in tone and tenure, from soft and reassuring, to tough and demanding. He tried to reassure the public while simultaneously congratulating himself. He did nothing to account for the circumstances they were now in or to address the loss of Task Force 31. The speech ended with his chief of staff, Cornelius Keyes clapping enthusiastically. It was not clear if the governor appreciated the interstellar politics or the import this would have for his future.

Gallant kept his distance throughout the event. But, afterward, when he had the governor in his stateroom, they spoke of the situation in terse terms. He presented the governor with several options for going forward. The governor chose to ignore them all. He let his own judgment lead. He discussed his plans for the next convoys.

Gallant said, "This year has been overloaded with misdirection, full of shiny promises you will never live up to."

Stein bristled.

"The war, the new genetic laws," said Gallant, "wherever you look, there are false hopes and broken dreams. Peace and prosperity were what the public wanted. It didn't happen. Instead, your misadventure has expanded the war. Now we are fighting our former ally."

"Don't speak to me like that," said Stein. "Look, I've had to deal with a difficult situation, but there was no other option. Don't you understand? You're a Natural. I'm afraid you don't understand."

"No. I don't. The convoys have been under constant harassment from hit and run raids. We've taken some hits. Thankfully, our losses so far have been light."

"You must go on escorting the convoys. I don't know what else I can say to convince you."

"You don't know how difficult the convoys are to maintain. If we must face the Great Ship, we will have to change our strategy."

"No. I have the final say," demanded Stein.

"Don't let your imagination catch fire. I made the situation clear."

Stein fidgeted, biting his nails. He didn't know a thing about military operations, but that didn't stop him from making demands. He stared as if considering Gallant's lack of response. There was something shifty in his eyes.

Stein said, "Maybe we could take some of the cruisers and destroyers off escort duty to hunt for the raiders. Or maybe send space trains without an escort. Enough might get through to meet the quota."

Gallant interpreted Stein's frequent complaints as a barometer of his apprehension.

Stein said, "Your success to date in moving convoys doesn't cover your failure to stop the Great Ship."

"I am accomplishing my mission bit by bit."

"I want the convoys kept safe."

"That could best be accomplished if you send a peace mission to the Chameleon," said Gallant. "If you offer reasonable terms to share the star system and stop fighting a former ally."

Stein looked like a naughty boy brought before the principal's office.

"After they destroyed Task Force 31, there can be no reconciliation."

Gallant considered his position. When you're in a critical situation, and someone else is holding the high cards, you may have to do things you don't like for people you don't trust. You don't always get to choose whom you do business with. Sometimes you are forced to make a deal with the devil.

Gallant said, "Opening a channel of communication with the Chameleon is vital to our long-term survival."

"I won't proceed."

"We had an agreement. I would protect the system while you undertook diplomatic relations."

Stein smirked. "May I give you a word of advice?"

Gallant remained quiet.

"Stick to flying your ship," said Stein. "Leave governing to those best qualified."

"Now, may I give *you* some advice."

"You may, but whether I heed it, is my prerogative. This job is full of tough choices."

Gallant got right into Stein's face and said,

"Put the welfare of your people first."

CHAPTER 8

Search

When Lorelei entered the *Constellation's* ready room, she was surprised to find Kelsey sitting in an empty corner of the compartment, shaking her head with her jaw clenched and her brows furrowed.

"What's wrong?" she asked.

"Henry, . . . err, Captain Gallant handed me a hot potato," said Kelsey. "He wants to upgrade the detection network to cover the entire star system. And he wants it done yesterday."

"Is it even possible to cover the entire star system?"

"No, it's not," said Kelsey, stamping her feet. "Not only that, but I'm supposed to coordinate surveillance with tracking any military response." She flailed her arms over her head. "How can I do all that? There are three convoys in progress at any one time, and perhaps a dozen Titan raider squadrons loose in the system."

Lorelei patted her on the shoulder. "Could you

use someone to bounce ideas off?"

"You'd better believe it," said Kelsey, heaving a sigh of relief.

Lorelei's face lit up. "Show me what you've got so far."

Handing her a tablet, Kelsey explained, "Our current network has failed to keep tabs on the Titan raiders that are harassing our convoys. I have to reassign the two hundred drones, twelve telescopic satellites, twenty sensor arrays, and twenty-four Hawkeyes."

She paused before adding, "I must keep most of the Hawkeyes for fleet protection. The other systems are passive devices that must be stationed efficiently. Then I must accumulate the data, correlate it, and distribute it to where it's needed. That means I have to account for relay delays in getting the target tracking information to the *Constellation*."

Lorelei examined the star system diagram. "You've got to prioritize. You'll have to pay particular attention to convoy routes and regions near the planets."

"I know . . ." Kelsey's voice trailed off. "Not only that, but I'll have to consider two completely different search methods. The Great Ship has almost perfect stealth while the Titan's stealth varies."

The two officers shared leadership responsibilities, as well as a personal friendship. But while Kelsey was grateful for the help, she was reluctant to admit her limitations. Nevertheless, working together over the next two hours, they managed to put together a coherent plan.

A great deal of exploration had been performed by robotic spacecraft missions already. The satellites were the workhorses of the grid system. The women decided to leave the satellites in place around the planets and the largest asteroids. They concentrated their attention on the other assets. They upgraded the drone coverage by allowing them to conduct box searches in regions ahead of convoys routes.

"Hopefully, we'll discover enemy operating areas before they can become a threat." Lorelei bit her lower lip. "Wait a minute; the XO should already have sighting reports. You need to integrate that information."

They continued working for another hour.

"You're leaving a lot to chance," said Lorelei.

Lorelei's attitude confused Kelsey. "It's a calculated risk-reward equation. We can't cover everything!"

"You'll have to get the XO's approval on this, and you know how the XO is," said Lorelei.

"We'll use Hawkeyes to scout the convoy paths. Others will spiral out from the task force to probe sightings."

"How about sending a few Hawkeye teams to deploy hidden detection arrays at critical points along the convoy routes?"

"Great idea," said Kelsey. "If we pick some possible vulnerable areas that might improve our odds."

They ran a series of simulations and correlated them with a statistical program to examine the overall coverage.

"It's a pathetic 4 percent coverage of the star system," said Kelsey. "Convoy routes are 17 percent covered, and the vicinities of planets are 23 percent."

"Still, that's nearly double what it was."

Kelsey grimaced. "That's all we can do with the resources we have. Unless you've got another idea?"

"Sorry I don't."

Kelsey hung her head. "The Great Ship and the Titan raiders can still set up bases in stealth mode and remain hidden until they choose to attack."

"I agree that this isn't going to make Captain Gallant happy, but we can only do the possible. We'll have to leave the impossible to him."

Their laughter echoed across the room.

CHAPTER 9

A Sitting Duck

Aurora smacked her hand on the table.
WHACK!
The Great Ship's captain flinched.
Aurora said, "Captain Falcon, your actions are unforgivable!"

"It was necessary," he shrugged. The Chameleon ambassador displeasure was anticipated, but her livid display was unexpected. He looked around the ambassador's suite for an exit, but several guards were in his way.

Aurora's olive-green eyes swept over the officer like a brush fire. "Destroying the human task force has started a war we neither wished nor were prepared for."

"They didn't accept the ultimatum," mumbled the officer.

She said, "We were still negotiating."

"Ha! They were already dispersing their task force. I had to make a split-second decision. They were a threat to this ship and its mission. They were all just sitting there together—a perfect target," he said, raising his eyebrows. "If I waited, we would have lost our great tactical advantage."

She said, "Our national doctrine is based on diplomacy. Over time, that would have brought them into an agreement to share the system. Now we are forced to make a hasty and fragile alliance with our archenemy, the Titan. How long do you think that will last?"

"We have great leverage over the humans," he said, producing a crooked smirk.

Aurora said, "I recognize the new task force in the system. They are more formidable. They have a powerful leader."

Raising his balled fist into the air, Falcon said, "I can deal with him."

"I don't think you realize how precarious our position is." Aurora's entire being roiled in changing colors, shifting from dark to light and back again.

The room remained deathly still for several minutes. Then Falcon lowered his head and opened his hands. "We will harass their convoys, and eventually, this will force them to a diplomatic solution to our advantage."

Aurora said, "I will try to open a dialog with the human, but I worry we will become entangled with the Titans."

"Leave the Titans to me. I know how to deal with them," said Falcon, puffing out his chest. "If they recognize an advantage to cooperating with us, they will jump at it."

"I fear we will face a fearful reckoning," said Aurora.

CHAPTER 10

The Lad

Gallant woke from a troubled sleep, his dreams filled with disturbing images of the dead and dying of Task Force 31. He immediately checked his bedside monitor for his ship's status and flipped through the survivors' medical reports. Rising, he felt renewed strength flow through his veins as he started his morning ritual. His mind was already teeming with ideas and possibilities as he drank his coffee on the bridge.

The OOD reported, "*Warrior* arriving, sir."

The arrival of the commanding officer of the *Warrior* was welcome news to Gallant. He couldn't wait to greet his old friend and receive a firsthand account of the ship's mission.

"Have him report to my cabin."

"Aye aye, sir."

A few minutes later, Captain Roberts said, "Reporting as ordered, sir."

"John, thank you for coming so promptly. I wanted to hear more about the *Warrior's* recent exploits."

Roberts smiled as they shook hands. "It'll be my pleasure."

They sat on the less than comfortable chairs in Gallant's small cabin.

Gallant said, "After I divided the task force into four strike groups, I hoped it would be enough to protect our convoys and keep an eye on the Great Ship. I wanted the *Warrior* to scout out the other side of the star system. I've read your report, but I'm glad to have an opportunity to hear from you directly."

"I traveled across the system, maintaining maximum stealth and collecting information," said Roberts. "The Titan raiders are in units of one cruiser and half-a-dozen destroyers. They travel along the convoy routes. I figure there are a dozen of these. The Titans have a base somewhere in the center of the asteroid belt they use for supplies and repairs. They poke and prod, looking for an opening to pick off a weak or damaged cargo vessel. The harassment is considerable, but the escorts are doing an admirable job protecting the convoys."

"What else have you seen?" asked Gallant.

"I also got a glimpse of the Great Ship near the planet Beta, two weeks ago. It took no offensive action, but it did exchange communication with one of the Titan squadrons."

Gallant listened while on the edge of his chair. "The governor is a problem. He wants to keep the convoys running and ship material back to Earth to fill Neumann's coffers. He isn't interested in negotiating with the Chameleon or the losses we may suffer as a result."

Roberts said, "We have to come up with a plan to limit the Great Ship's range of operation and eventually find a way to neutralize or destroy it. Its stealth and shield strengths are remarkable."

"I have initiated a research team to investigate methods to offset the Great Ship's advantages. They are operating out of a bunker on Charlie."

"I hope they can succeed" Roberts said. "The combined Chameleon and Titan threat is formidable. Task Force 34 is being pulled in too many directions. Wouldn't it be better to keep the task force intact?"

"I would if I could, but the commercial shipping would be devastated by the Titan raiders. The Titans threatened convoys bound for Charlie, and they tie-down our assets."

"It was not just a matter of size or sheer numbers. Strength is not measured by such things alone. We have excellent, well-trained crews. I'll match our skill against the enemy any day."

"That's true," said Gallant. "But the Great Ship is a monster with those protruding spikes seventy kilometers long. It's mindboggling."

"It's not all-powerful, or the Titan wouldn't have destroyed most of them. There was only one left, and it can't be both protecting its home and attacking us. It must have limitations in power and ability, and it's up to us to discover them."

The conversation droned on for several more minutes until they finally ran out of professional topics.

Roberts bit his lip.

Silence hung heavy in the room, but Gallant was reluctant to let his friend go.

He said, "I visited the hospital and spoke to the survivors from Task Force 31. It was hard to hear about their wounds and their tales of suffering."

"Give them time," said Roberts.

Gallant played with a button on his uniform, twirling it back and forth.

"There was one young man in a coma," said Gallant, a prickle of defensiveness, doused with a measure of guilt crawled up his spine.

"I spent an hour reading his favorite book to him. It was called *War and Peace*, written hundreds of years ago." As a survivor of many battles, Gallant had sat dolefully beside the dying man. "I think it did me more good than him."

"*War and Peace*, that's a lofty title."

"Yes, so it is. It's about a people full of joy and prosperity," said Gallant, "until war brings them suffering and death."

"Humph. Not much has changed. Has it?"

Gallant looked away, "Guess not."

"Is there anything more that can be done for the lad?" asked Roberts

"I'm dealing with it," said Gallant. "I left instructions to keep me informed of his condition."

"When will he recover?"

"Oh, you know."

"Roger that."

CHAPTER 11

The Lie Inside the Lie

"You, lying bastard!"

Kate's explosion startled Logan.

"You, lying sack of shh...," she screamed. Embarrassment and anger crept up her neck in hot pricks. "You found the key to this puzzle on your last simulation, and you said nothing."

She pointed to his computer monitor, which exposed the truth.

Logan preened. "Puzzles often have unexpected solutions, just like detective stories may have unexpected villains."

Her eyes bulged. "You're a *poseur*."

"Okay. I got lucky. I made a wild guess, and it paid off."

"Listen," she said, but the outside howling became a distracting whisper.

A small treacherous part of her hoped he'd confess that he only found the key because of her analysis.

"The truth is," he said, "I used the AI to speculate on some parameter options that you identified. Then I just took a wild guess. I'm as shocked as you are that it yielded a real possibility."

Kate's shoulders sagged as she visibly calmed down. She sighed in resignation.

"No," she admitted. "You showed real skill in selecting that parameter set. I acknowledge your talent."

Logan gave a nonchalant shrug, but his smug grin remained.

"Calling you a *poseur*. Not cool," she said. "Congratulations on finding the key to the first puzzle. I apologize for insulting you."

"That's okay. Apology accepted," said Logan sympathetically. "This puts us one step closer to a solution for the Great Ship's stealth capability. We still need to test it. That will require many more quantum computer simulations. Thousands, maybe, before we can believe it."

"Cool," she said. "It's just that I've been working so hard, day and night. I didn't think anyone could crack this puzzle faster than I could. I totally freaked out. Sorry. I mean, I guess sometimes brute force logic *is* better than subtle creativity."

"As I said, it wasn't all logic. I made a lucky guess. We can still be friends, right?"

"Yeah. Sure." But then she leaned forward and got into his face and said, "But we're competitors, you know."

"Fine, if that's the way you prefer to work."

"Sometimes, I ramble when I get nervous." She

took a breath. "Okay, now tell me exactly how you discovered this key."

"It was all about sorting through the details of the parameter set you identified." He showed her the computer readout. "What I found was an anomaly pattern in the Great Ship's stealth performance. There is a side effect of the technology that produces a halo that our AI sensors can detect if they're tuned to the correct visible light frequencies."

She nodded as she scanned his computer screen output.

"I ran simulations for several different problems under your protocol. And I've developed several software tools to use as short cuts. I'm sure you would have gotten to the same results before long," he concluded.

"Don't patronize me. I've worked on these artifacts for months before you came. I didn't find that pattern. But your data is only a few points at one range and angle to our sensors. We need to run thousands of simulations examining many variations before this is a practical solution."

Logan quietly hummed a tune while flipping through the info. "We can do the simulations to learn as much as possible, but I'm confident they will verify my findings."

"This is all new territory."

Logan said, "Listen, I admit I had some advantages, but it came down to pure luck in breaking the Chameleon encrypted signal processing system. Plus, your suggestion on how to program it all on the quantum supercomputer put me over the top."

Kate stared at him. Her jealousy vanished, replaced by genuine admiration. Finally, she sighed, "Okay."

She plugged her flash drive into his tablet and swiped a few commands.

"Hey! What are you doing?" said Logan.

She did a complete download that snatched all his personal software shortcut tools and data into her folder.

"Come on, that's cheating."

"No, it's not," said Kate. "Now we're even. Competition brings out the beast in me. Now that I know you're a serious rival. I wouldn't let up."

Logan folded his arms. "Neither will I."

"Good. I'm ambitious too." Kate said, "Our next step is to program the neural nets of the quantum supercomputer to test your Halo Effect Theory. The effectiveness of the Chameleon stealth will prove to be a lie because we can see inside it to detect their ship."

Kate found herself at the computer console deep in thought about how to program the neural nets. Logan helped identify the key frequencies.

The data was displayed on the right of the screen, and the critical evaluation was shown on a three-dimensional plot in the lower-left corner. Keeping an eye on the behavior of the stimulus, Kate used her peripheral vision to watch the computer's response.

Behind her, a cacophony of computer sounds,

and beeps popped up. She noticed her reflection in the console glass, but the distortion troubled her. She'd spent years working on complex puzzles. Never once did she imagine this involvement. It was an awesome challenge. The repetitive electronic bleeps of the simulation tallied up the score. All their studies and preparation paid off.

She pondered what to do next. A path appeared in the pattern for her to follow. Her mind raced as she progressed. The AI constantly overwrote her software efforts with syntax corrections. She didn't mind at first, but when it started showing suggested code on the display, she turned it off.

"How much longer?" asked Logan.

"Don't worry about me; speed is my specialty," said Kate. She worked across the network and helped him maneuver through the maze of data. "My code will detect the stealth halo."

An hour later, she said, "Got it! Here are the results."

Logan copied the key onto a flash drive.

She didn't look so unhappy anymore. Now she was beaming. "There are still lots of secrets to unmask."

Logan said, "You realize what this means? Captain Gallant expects more from you since you're the expert. I'll get an easy pass."

"I'm dying to talk to someone about our progress so far. I can't wait to transmit this information to Captain Gallant."

Logan said, "I've completed a preliminary report to send to the *Constellation*. I'll send it as soon as you review it."

That made Kate anxious.

CHAPTER 12

Prey for Us

The Titan cruiser floated in the void, under cloak. It hovered in the darkest blackest corner of space while the starfield rotated behind it. Only its passive sensors probed around it. Like a prowling wolf, the cruiser waited for prey to wander across its path. The methane-breathing creatures inside listened, watched and waited. Unique genetic engineering had created these intelligent beings, but they were bereft of empathy or compassion.

Finally, the drifting warship caught a trace of an energy source. The stranger's energy emissions were a bright beacon beckoning the cruiser. The Titan commander reoriented his sensors to focus on the signature of the vessel. He knew his foe, and while he respected their resilience, he enjoyed the kill.

"Anything there?" asked Captain Martha Erskine of the space tug *Ulysses*.

The sensor operator said, "I thought for a second... no its nothing. Just my imagination, Captain."
Erskine turned to the communications officer and asked, "Any word from the convoy?"
"No, Captain."
"How far to the rendezvous point?"
The navigator said, "At this speed, we'll be there in thirty hours, Ma'am."
Erskine frowned. She hated this. The late cargo loading had put her space tug behind schedule. Now she was racing to catch the convoy. It was dangerous.
For months, convoys had crisscrossed the star system bringing minerals from the planets to Charlie. One convoy had already been sent to Earth. The convoys traveled against a background of blistering solar flares. They persevered through asteroid passages despite the difficulty of making course corrections.
Drones and sensor arrays kept a constant vigil through the star system. They hoped to transmit early warning of lurking enemy danger, but the uncertainty tested the crew's character.
As the day passed, the sensor operator reported the detection of a stray erratic signal.
"They're always out there, somewhere," said the sensor operator.
"Yeah," said the communicator. "Rumor has it a Titan squadron bombarded planet Alpha. Last week, one space train was destroyed by a raider before it could join a convoy."
"Don't get all upset," said Erskine. She swal-

lowed her saliva. "We're doing just fine."

The sensor operator said, "Huh, Captain, I'm picking up a signal."

"Let me see."

"It looks like a military-grade engine drive," said the sensor operator.

They watched the signal grow stronger and closer. Soon it was on an intercept course. There could be no doubt.

"It's a Titan cruiser, Captain,"

"It's been stalking us all along," said the navigator.

Captain Martha Erskine nodded. She didn't expect mercy.

CHAPTER 13

Walkabout

Events were moving fast. So fast that Gallant had to work hard to keep a firm grip on them. Convoys and escorts were dispatched and monitored. Drones and Hawkeyes were released throughout the star system. Sensor arrays were deployed. Gallant examined every action report and every enemy sighting. He followed the course vectors of the Titan ships and searched relentlessly for a clue of the Great Ship's whereabouts.

He wanted to let his mind grapple with strategic and tactical ideas, but today he began his morning walk with the XO at his side. He disliked innovation being introduced into his habits, but Fletcher had expressed concern about the tense atmosphere in the ship. It seemed only a sensible step to gauge the crew's morale now that so much had changed.

As Gallant and the XO went from compartment to compartment, they observed the crew going about their duties. He saw one sailor sitting peacefully on the deck, welding a pipe. The sailor pulled his eyes up long enough to acknowledge them. He worked in the comfortable rhythm of someone familiar with hard work, but there were faint, unhappy lines gathered around his mouth that aged him.

Turning around, they went into the next compartment. The below decks watch saluted them. Gallant's eyes wandered over a pressure manifold and glanced at the normal readings. He squeezed by a repair team moving along the passage. Generally, rank has its privilege going up and down ladders, with juniors yielding to seniors. The same goes for narrow passages. They made way for their seniors in the cramped three-dimensional environment. The crew looked up to see who might be in the way and observed proper military courtesy.

Gallant opened an airtight hatch and continued into a side passage followed by the XO.

Petty Officer Third Class Andy Flint was a capable electrician—when he was pressed to obey orders. He was working on an electrical a junction box but had haphazardly spread his gear out on the deck, blocking the passage. Barely a scrap of a man, he was young and dark-complexioned. He was always getting into trouble on liberty for fighting and drinking. The XO had disciplined him several times.

Gallant stood patiently for a moment, before asking, "How are you today, Flint?"

"Fine, Captain. I'm doing some maintenance replacing fuses," he made no effort to move his gear to clear the passage. "Just a typical day."

A typical day in a sailor's life sounds like a bit

of an oxymoron because there isn't anything familiar about it while you're in a war zone. But there are a few things to count on. Stuff will break, the work will need to be done, and chiefs will never be satisfied. Sailors are exposed to a variety of different work environments on the ship. Responsibilities are highly specialized. The various departments focus on their duties, whether they're on the flight deck or hangar deck, in the combat information center, or in a reactor room. There is a great deal of work to be done at any given time, so sailors are kept busy.

Every different rate has a different job. Everybody has his own specialty, their own work, their own responsibilities. The work varies from nuclear, to mechanic, to electricians, to weapons techs, and more. At the same time, everybody stands watch, and everybody adheres to the meal schedule, everybody participated in the drills, and everybody has a part to play for battle stations or emergencies. Living for six months or more with hundreds of people means close quarters and a lot of patience and camaraderie. The circumstances also require complete, unwavering loyalty and obedience to the ship's captain. That's how a sailor is forged.

"Have you served on other ships?" asked Gallant.

"No, sir. Just the *Constellation*," said Flint. The man's eyes remained narrow and suspicious; a pair of damp blue orbs set in deep crevasses. They could swallow you whole or burn you with their stare.

"Do you feel well-trained to do your job?"

"Yes, sir."

"Are you working to improve your rating?"

"Nah," said Flint, shaking his head.

Most sailors could expect promotions to petty officer within the first year of service. With hard work and good behavior, a sailor could expect regular promotion up the ratings. Flint's behavior resulted in being busted down to basic, more than once. He had lost his enthusiasm to move up again.

"Are you getting enough sleep?"

"Nah."

"What seems to be your problem?"

"If the navy paid more attention to sailors' job satisfaction and motivation, then a lot of other issues would fix themselves," he said. "Navy leaders have to want to transform the culture. This change cannot be forced down. It must grow from the ground up."

That was not the reaction Gallant expected. He worried that sleep deprivation might lead to mental health issues.

Fletcher said, "Leave this to me, sir."

Gallant nodded, and they resumed their journey.

In the next, compartment they talked to another crewman. "My name is Rawlings, third class, gunners' mate, sir." His eyes lit up like a neon sign. Rawlings was transferred to the ship just before they left port. He joined the space force eighteen years ago and said the only thing he didn't love about the service was being away from family. He loved the camaraderie and fraternal environment and shared advice.

Gallant joined Fletcher and the officers in the wardroom. The off-duty officers sat close together chatting.

"I want to congratulate the officers and crew on a fine operation" said Gallant.

He threw the meeting open to discussion. The officers expressed concern about the safety of the ship and crew. One officer lamented that there was still not consistent training to enable men and women to master various jobs. An officer said that the promised reforms aimed at improving training overtaxed service members.

Then the officers began talking about their social life as much as their professional duties. They represented people from many planets. They understood about deployments, having to wake up early, and the other pressures and oddities of military life. But whether those who socialized were military, one thing was certain. It was just easier to socialize with buddies aboard ship.

Friendships were apparent, but underlying stress simmered.

CHAPTER 14

The Halo Effect

The full ramifications of Logan's success hit Kate's ego hard. She was determined to win their competition by solving the next puzzle. That got her moving.

After sending their preliminary report to the *Constellation,* they ran additional quantum supercomputer simulations for hours to verify Logan's theory.

She lost track of time over the next few days until, at last, they were ready to compare the thousand simulation runs and glean out the conclusions. Kate found herself standing alone in the corner of the room. In her palm was a flash drive loaded with data. She was overcome with wonder and elation about what they might find. She turned it over in her hand. She watched the light shine off its metallic surface. She reviewed the data results on the computer screen. They were conclusive.

Logan said, "This confirms our theory about a detectable halo effect."

The fact that he called it "our theory" wasn't lost on Kate.

She looked over the statistical analysis of the 1000 simulations they had run on her quantum supercomputer. She nodded in the affirmative. "This is conclusive. We have a way of detecting the Great Ship at reasonable distances with an acceptable probability. I'm satisfied that the software works and is ready for installation."

"The AI sensors will be able to kinda identify that the stealth technology produces a halo that shimmers around the Great Ship," said Logan. "We can get a glimpse of it in motion. This is enough to change the Chameleon's stealth advantage."

Kate said, "We need to transmit the Halo Effect information to Captain Gallant. We can include the AI software package for the sensor array."

"Yes. He can install the software for the sensor array on the *Constellation*. I'll prepare a direct beam transmission."

"Okay. Then we can get started on the next puzzle," said Kate. "And I'm going to beat you to the next key."

"I welcome the competition," said Logan.

Kate wasn't getting any sleep tonight.

CHAPTER 15

Goliath

When Ryan arrived on the flight deck, the crew chief handed him a tablet with outstanding flight issues on his Viper. He shook his head. The list was long. He swiped past his ship's status and began a disheartening examination of the rest of his flight. There were starfighters in even worse shape. He checked the flight manifest and the fuel load before takeoff.

The preflight briefing was quick. The Vipers were brought up from the hangers below. The situation became stressed as the launch window narrowed. On the flight deck, the crew chiefs faced the test. The flight control officer scheduled a maximum effort operation.

Caked with dried oil and grime from continuous hard use, Ryan's Viper, known as 'Lucky 7,' was streaked with laser burns and plasma blisters. In the immediate atmosphere of quiet efficiency, the starfighter's cockpit was in disorder. A bedlam of minor alarms, out-of-spec noises, flashing yellow warning lights as systems came online. There were computer systems booting up, "check temperature" warnings, pressures, and energy readings. The fighter was scheduled for refit and long-overdue upgrades.

Ryan sighed.

What can I do?

Scrubbing the problematic ships would overburden the rest.

What was fair about that?

The squadron was keeping a lookout for the Great Ship and chasing Titan raiders.

The enemy was somewhere, but *where?*

Simultaneously, they were presented with a significant threat and an opportunity. Destroying the Great Ship would be a magnificent victory. It would keep their stars safe and lifelines open. If they failed, they would be paralyzed by the peril.

Ryan's fighter was hauled into the launch skid by a tractor. The starfighters began to launch.

In the past few days, the bomber squadrons prepared to use the new Goliath missiles. They were specially constructed weapons designed against the Great Ship. The first problem was how to piggyback the huge weapon on the existing starfighter. Fitting the huge weapons onto the Viper II was difficult. The greater payload meant additional training for the pilots. Once they mastered the new weapon, they faced the problem of delivering them.

The bombers had trained to deliver one hell of a wallop. They passed space trails and were being armed for the real thing. They would have to travel fast enough and far enough to deliver a bang big enough to make their sacrifice worthwhile.

The pilots had just completed training exercises with the warheads attached amidships. The first pair had launched safely. The fourth team hit difficulties and set off an alarm. They managed to prevent premature detonation. The effort proved the concept was workable. As the launch continued, an accident occurred, and the death of one pilot slowed things down.

.

CHAPTER 16

A Spark in the Dark

The SIA bunker on Charlie was full of covert operators, analysts, and technicians decrypting and translating alien communications. Some were engaged in detecting and tracking alien ships. Critical information updates were broadcast to the Constellation. In one basement laboratory, a few techs worked with Kate and Logan, examining the Great Ship's super-laser technology.

"You found the key to the stealth puzzle."

"Kate," said Logan, a hurt look on his face, "we did that together. I thought you were over that."

She shrugged. "It's a process."

"After the adrenaline rush of a win comes an emotional crash," said Logan. "It takes a little while to build up a head of steam again. So, show some team spirit."

She cringed at the admonishment and reluctantly said, "Okay. Now let's find the key to the super-laser power technology."

A veiled background noise whispered around

them then grew louder. It was as if the world began to whisper to her, then call her.

What was its message? Kate wondered. "Did you hear that?"

"It's just the wind howling outside," said Logan.

"No. This was different. I swear it was a voice."

"What did it say?"

"I'm not sure, but it sounded like... *beware.*"

"You're messing with me again."

She stared. "Forget it."

Logan said, "Let's get back to work."

He pulled up the working file for the superlaser on his tablet. "The burst of energy from that massive weapon is like a volcano shot in space. What's its energy source?"

She said, "Let's not imagine a brand-new technology leapfrogging our science to create so much power. Let's go old school. Let's assume they used ordinary means and scaled it up. Perhaps 1000 fission-fusion reactors would be powerful enough."

"Wow. That's a great idea. The Chameleon think big. That's why they built the Great Ship."

Kate and Logan donned their immersive VR suits and entered the Great Ship virtual reality. While the Great Ship was a hundred kilometers long, the wonderful thing about the VR was that their avatars could 'fly' its length in a matter of minutes.

Logan made his way to the weapons power location. The instant he got there, he crawled through a tunnel. It was a null-connectivity zone, so he was out of contact from Kate. She was exploring the ship's engines. He pulled out his map and comm pin. Clues were sparse, but you could do much if you knew where to look and had good instincts. When he got through, he found that Kate had left a dozen messages.

Kate said, "We've got the recorded data from the Great Ship's rescue of Ryan's starfighters during the battle in the Gliese star system. It recorded the Great Ship firing its laser."

"But we can't solve the formulas. They are too non-linear and interactive," said Logan. "Way beyond our analytical calculus capabilities."

"You're right. We can't solve those equations," said Kate, examining the power-frequency curve. "We need to reduce the problem into something manageable. Let's start with a first-order differential equation which we *can* solve. Let's try to find the key to this puzzle by making a spark in the dark."

"A spark?"

"Well, I'm talking relative to the super-laser." Kate said, "If we can't develop new math to solve the Great Ship's power curve, then let's use old math. Make a simplifying assumption and use rough approximation. We could use the differential equations for the *Constellation's* laser. We know how to solve those. We can treat use finite element analysis to approximate the collected data. Once we have that, we can try to scale it."

"Hmm," said Logan.

Kate said, "That would be good enough if we

use the super quantum computer. We may be able to simulate the Chameleon's technology with those approximations."

Logan said, "That might work. We could build test devices with those approximations."

After several days, Kate said, "My simulations show a Hawking's blackholes effect; emitting thermal radiation proportional to mass."

Logan flipped through the channels and examined her results. He said, "I don't know about this."

"I've had several false starts, but I think I'm making progress on the equations," said Kate. Her idea of using old school approximations as a spark was working and producing results.

Logan wasn't as impressed with himself now that Kate had possibly found the key to solving the second puzzle. Like everyone else, he was waiting for her next step.

"Cut it out, okay? It's not really a big deal. You haven't won yet," Logan said in frustration.

Kate said, "I know. I've got to convert my raw data into real facts." Anyone smart enough to accomplish what she had, knows better than to risk everything with premature claims.

"I'm going to read these clues for the thousandth time. To check," said Logan.

"Thanks."

Kate slept for twelve hours straight after several grueling days, but she was convinced she had done it. When she finally woke up, she rubbed her eyes and lay silently for a while, trying to convince herself that she had succeeded, and it was not all a dream. She had scored a major victory in breaking a puzzle piece. She was even with him now.

If you miss your moment, it's gone, she thought. Kate scolded, "You've only got yourself to blame. I told you I was a serious competitor. You should have taken me more seriously. Did you think you could get lightning to strike twice? You were so smug after solving the first key. Now you've learned your place. Instead of buckling down and focusing on the quest, you idled away your time."

"I wasn't idle. I was working as hard as you. I'm just not as good at solving differential equations."

"You need to get your head back in the game. Now that I've found the second key, we need to verify it and send the information to Captain Gallant."

Logan said, "We have three prizes to collect: the secret to each of stealth, super-lasers, and shields. Once we have them, we can destroy the Great Ship. I solved the stealth key. Now you've solved the laser key. We still have the hardest puzzle left."

"True. And I'm going to beat you to it," she said confidently.

"Yeah, but first, we have to send this information to Captain Gallant."

She said, "I'd like to include an extra little nugget I found."

"What's that?"

Kate snapped her fingers and leaned forward as if to reveal a great secret. "I've been solving mysteries at SAI's Bletchley Circle for years, but this has been extra gratifying."

She paused, pleased to see the anticipation on Logan's face.

"Solving the power distribution system of the Great Ship has yielded something especially useful," she said. "Based on the simulations I've run, I discovered a vulnerability in the power system that *only exists after it fires its super-laser*. At that time, the ship's power is so depleted that its shield strength will be down to a trickle. If a missile hits the ship in the right spot, it could do serious damage to the ship's reactors. It could put the ship out of action for a considerable time. The Great Ship would have to limp along until it was repaired."

"Great find. I'll include that information in our transmission," said Logan. Then he sighed and squinted as he asked, "If you don't like working with me, why do you do it?"

"The devil you know. You know?"

"Yeah. I get it. Crazy is crazy."

SISSSSS!

A distracting distant noise startled them.

Kate starred at the wall.

Why is it that just when you think you've got things figured out, someone pitches you a curveball? She wondered.

The rustling noise from outside continued. It was like a faraway voice, a whisper.

What is it saying? Kate wondered, *what does it know?*

Kate shut her eyes tight and concentrated on

the sound. Everything seemed dull gray like in a mystery story.

Was it real?

She nursed the hope that the whispers would tell her a secret.

There was a momentary silence while she thought about it. There were times when she felt the world was too big for her, that she was too small.

"What's the matter with you?" asked Logan.

"Hush. I'm listening."

A bitter taste in her mouth made her swallow. She had a strange intuitive feeling about the whispering. She knew it would still be there when she opened her eyes.

"What are you doing?" Logan chuckled, "If you keep this up, your overindulgent imagination is going to conjure up monsters from your ID."

Kate opened her eyes. It felt like lasers were shining into them.

CHAPTER 17

Wakeup

Task Force 34.4 escorted a gigantic convoy of space trains on course to Charlie. One destroyer squadron surrounded the convoy as close support. The rest were on a parallel course just behind.

Gallant smiled as he read the OOD's latest entry in the *Constellation's* log, "As before, conditions normal, ahead standard." He flipped back to the previous page, which was chocked full of a more realistic picture of daily activities aboard ship. This included routine maintenance and repairs interspersed invectives of crewmen being injured either by malfunctioning equipment or careless acts. One entry read, "Crewman Joseph slipped on a foreign substance and accidentally fell off a catwalk." The entry failed to report that the substance was grease carelessly dropped by a workman.

Pacing, back and forth, along the starboard wing of the bridge, was one of Gallant's favorite habits. He could lose himself in thought, playing out a variety of battle scenarios. Because his adversary was not only powerful but also wily, he had CIC run extensive simulations—there would be no opportunity for second chances. He hoped for warning through his extensive search and detection grid that Kelsey had established. That, along with the Halo Effect software that Logan and Kate had transmitted, were his main buttresses.

There were many reports of Titan cruiser-destroyer squadrons conducting swift raids. So far, the damage had not been severe, but tension ran high throughout the star system. The only thing was to fight past any raiders. No convoy ships had been lost. But there were delays and many accidents. The Great Ship appeared only once near a planet, and it caused consternation.

He thought about sending an alert to the convoy, but what more could he add to the existing warnings, which were to beware and obey orders.

The OOD reported, "No contacts, sir."

"Very Well," said Gallant.

He planned to doggedly plod on through any obstacle hoping every member of the convoy did his best to bear their responsibility as part of the whole.

There was no contact for now. He could make a slight course adjustment that would move them from the know convoy route. The bridge crew remained at their stations, working diligently. They ignored their commanding officer's peccadilloes.

"Officer of the Deck, change convoy course five degrees to starboard."

"Aye aye, sir."

Gallant considered how far off the optimized trajectory this would place the convoy. Perhaps it would avoid a specific trap laid by the enemy.

It wasn't long after they settled on the new heading that he heard, "Contact, bearing 010, range indefinite."

"Get a fix on that," he told them.

"Trying, sir, but the signal is weak and uncertain."

If this were a Titan raider, he would try to find an opening to approach the convoy out of range of the escorts. Three-dimensional space meant that the raider could approach from many directions, and the escorts had to cover them all. Gallant had to decide if he should send an escort to chase the contact and leave a gap in the convoy coverage.

"Lost contact, sir."

No sense sending a destroyer to track that down, he thought.

Soon, the report came, "no contacts."

An hour later, there came, "Contact, bearing 010, range indefinite."

Gallant was sure now. They were baiting him, staying at extreme range, and letting him get a whiff. Then they would scramble away, hoping he would send escorts and give them an opening. Well, he wouldn't oblige.

Soon another contact was reported, this time to port. The situation repeated itself over the next six hours with minor variations. The temptation was to chase the enemy raiders or at least send his CSP, which was equally unsatisfactory.

"All contacts lost, sir."

The before long, "Contact bearing 010, range ten light-minutes."

They held contact for several minutes, and he watched the plot.

"OOD, vector the CSP to the contact," said Gallant.

"Aye aye, sir."

The CSP reported, "Target is a Titan destroyer. Request permission to attack."

"There he is, the bugger," exclaimed the chief.

It was too tempting, and Gallant accepted the challenge.

"Permission granted."

The explosions of missiles on target were silent in space but lit up the monitor well enough. The raider was quickly dispatched.

"We got him, sir. Got him good."

"That's fine," said Gallant. "Great! Well done."

"Picking up debris at the last point of contact, sir."

The whole ship reveled in the small victory. A lighthearted atmosphere prevailed on the bridge.

"We got that S.O.B.," said an operator.

Only a few minutes later, there was a report, "Contact, bearing 330, range ten light-minutes."

There it was. His CSP was now on the other side of the convoy. They could help if this was a more serious attack.

"OOD, launch the standby fighter."

He could shore things up a little. His hands were stiff. He flexed them back and forth. Watching the monitor, he sipped his coffee while the convoy proceeded on course in a steady fashion.

Soon the CSP was back on station, and the contact disappeared once more.

"Sir, we have a communication from the space tug *Star Rover*. For Captain's eyes only."

"I'll read it here," he said, indicating to his command console.

A glance was enough to see it was a complaint and a demand for better protection with closer support.

Gallant calculated that the enemy was on each side of the convoy. He deduced a vague sense of their tactics and position. He considered where they might take a chance to strike at escorts to create an opening for other raiders.

Before long, one Titan did approach the destroyer *Leone* and launched a missile salvo at extreme range. There was little chance the missiles would survive the countermeasures and antimissiles, but it forced the *Leone* out of position.

The CIC officer reported, "Unrecognized signal coming from ahead, sir."

"Is it a stealth anomaly?" asked Gallant.

The OOD said, "Possibly, sir. It shows a distorted glow pattern."

The Bletchley Circle software was installed on the *Constellation's* sensors. This might be an early detection of the Great Ship's Halo Effect. The starfighters were instructed to strike at vulnerable areas on the Great Ship if they got the chance.

"Where the hell is that ship?" muttered Gallant.

The XO said, "Something's brewing. I can feel it."

"Course and speed of the target?" asked Gallant.

"Not yet, sir. But it's one light-hour distance."

"Track it and keep me updated."

"Aye aye, sir."

Gallant switched to the task force communication channel. He said, "All ships sound general quarters."

He ordered the *Constellation* and two destroyers to take a new heading at right angles to the unknown anomaly. He ordered the battlecruisers and the remaining destroyers to spread out.

After several minutes, he ordered a destroyer squadron to diverge from the battlecruisers.

They waited for the shimmering glimpse of the Great Ship to reappear.

Gallant hoped these preparations were enough to meet the danger. He didn't want to be too provocative, but he did want to be ready for anything.

The CIC officer reported, "Halo signal, bearing 040 range ten light-minutes, sir."

"OOD, order the convoy to scatter."

The OOD used the battle command datalink to direct each ship according to a prearranged dispersal pattern. Gallant waited hands clenched into white knuckle fists before the first space tug began to turn.

The convoy followed the prescribed scattering plan. The long columns of vessels were succeeding in avoiding collisions and expanding the diameter of the convoy.

Gallant hoped that the convoy presented an unappealing target.

And then it happened.

The world changed, shifting with shocking suddenness. The void of space before the *Constellation* wiggled, and blackness devoured the stars.

The Great Ship materialized. Its super-laser tube was pointing in the general direction of the task force.

Oh no!

Gallant instinctively gripped his chair and held his breath as the endless wall of steel materialized.

The chief-of-the-watch pulled a lever, and the *Constellations* collision alarm wailed.

CLANG! CLANG! CLANG!

The din was enough to tense every muscle, enough to summon the crew to their posts. The danger was real and ahead, and there was no help coming.

The ship was pulsating with excitement and activity.

The chief of the watch announced, "Now hear this! Now hear this! Standby for radical maneuvering."

He heard the Great Ship order, "United

Planets' ships we demand your surrender."

The chief of the watch announced, "Take precautions against radiation exposure."

Anxiety grabbed at him.

But he wasn't afraid to face danger.

Gallant yelled, "Hard to port!"

The OOD said, "Deploy drones and decoys."

Seconds passed as they changed direction so that *Constellation's* course became perpendicular to the line of fire of the great weapon.

Minutes passed as they moved away from the barrel of the huge cannon.

He hoped the task force would spread out enough to get clear.

How much time do I have? he wondered.

As the ships of Task Force 34 executed his orders—he waited.

Over the next several seconds, he concentrated on avoiding the path of the blast.

How long would the Chameleon wait before shooting?

In the first seconds, he watched the monitor, and the tracking vectors as the chest-crushing g's began.

The next seconds, he fought down the concern as the ships increased 20 g's tested the limitations.

Then, he felt as if he feared it was all for naught.

Several seconds later, he blinked against the glare of the sun. Even as he turned his ship, he heard

Fletcher gasp, "We can't ... make it ..."

HISS! CRACKLE! SIZZLE!

A tremendous burst of hellish energy flowed out of the super-laser. It was a brilliant orange-red eruption, so bright and strange and exotic that Gallant wanted to stare at it and shield his eyes at the same time.

It's as if space itself is on fire, he thought.

He felt the splash of fire and heat as the humming lightning bolt pulsed near his ship. And in the blink of an eye, the beam was gone. Only a glowing ember at the end of the seventy-kilometer tube remained

Someone is tugging at my arm. Perhaps the OOD is summoning me to the bridge. I must have overslept, thought Gallant.

A harsh breeze brought the smell of pungent fumes. His lungs strained to inhale the wispy air, but he could only draw-in an empty gulp. His heart pounded.

A loud hiss of escaping air trickled out of the compartment. Faint echoes of whining machinery pleaded for attention. Steam rolled out of a pipe, coiling and writhing like a snake climbing into the air.

"I can't breathe!" squeaked from his mouth.

As Gallant drifted back into a deep fog, fumes covered his nose and mouth. Despite the burning material, the cold of space enveloped him. It was like being submerged in a frozen river. An incalculable weight pressed downward, seemingly dragging him under. It seemed easier to let the river take him.

Finally, fresh air flowed into the compartment. His chest rose with a precious breath. The visceral fear of suffocation receded. With stiff fingers, he massaged his numb arms and legs. His fingernails dug deep into his palms. His body felt fragile and weak.

"Owww."

Was that me?

"Captain Gallant! Captain Gallant!"

Someone was shaking him.

"Please, wake up! We need you!"

Gallant reluctantly opened his eyes, but his head was dizzy, and the room was spinning. His tunnel vision blurred from vertigo and nausea. He shook his head, and he opened his eyes wide, trying to make sense of the dark shapes around him.

Where am I?

Cold sweat and warm blood soaked his uniform. There were only the emergency lights.

A voice said, "This will help."

Someone jabbed him with a needle. After a minute, his head still throbbed, but the room had stopped spinning.

"Captain Gallant," said a young man beside him, shaking him once more.

He had awakened almost every morning in the last decade of his life in a tiny grey room in a spaceship traveling between stars. The sounds and smells had always been familiar ones. But this was different. But at this moment, he didn't know where he was. His consciousness reverted to reality like a light flicked on by a switch.

He was lying on the deck of the bridge. He lay there in a fog in the mentally in-between state of consciousness of dreams and reality.

He hoped he would wake soon because his dream was the most unpleasant one that he'd ever experienced. His body was floating amongst dead bodies and wreckage. There's a deafening racket to his right and scorching heat to his left. He was having a dreadful time breathing—for all that—he couldn't rouse himself to open his eyes.

He brought his legs under him and attempted to stand. His entire body hurt, but slowly he managed to force himself erect. His spaghetti strength legs wobbled, and his chest heaved against his navy-blue uniform. There was the taste of copper in his mouth and the smell of burning in the air. He swallowed the sour saliva. Despite all this, he believed he would be saved as faithfully as he believed in gravity.

There was something he wanted but couldn't have. It was something important but beyond his grasp. He wanted to go back to sleep and let this dream pass him by.

Then he remembered.

The Great Ship had fired its super-laser cannon.

I'm still alive. How is that possible? he thought. *Oh! That's right; I had a plan, a trap.*

A good trap doesn't make the enemy suspicious. It makes them curious. Curious enough to poke their nose into the hornet's nest.

Did it work?

As Gallant struggled to get his mind straight, he remembered the shimmering Halo image that betrayed the Great Ship. He recalled taking actions to prepare the convoy and task force. When the Great Ship dropped its stealth, the task force was already fully alert and moving to scatter. When it fired, it ignored the convoy. Instead, it targeted the battlecruiser *Invincible* and the nearby *Constellation*.

It scored a direct hit on the *Invincible* and a destroyer squadron, but only a near-miss against the *Constellation*.

The super-laser had exploded near the *Constellation's* hull. A radiation shock wave hit the ship, traveling so fast that there was no warning, and the crew was knocked about. It caused rents in the titanium steel forward of the midship frame. The radiation penetrated deep inside the ship. An explosion caused a fire in the galley, crew's quarters, and the second and third decks. There was structural damage and ruptured bulkheads and sprung hatches. A secondary explosion from flammable material caused splinters and fragments. More fires wounded many. This represented a considerable loss of hull integrity and combat readiness. The ship's armor was effective in protecting the engine and reactor compartments. Another splattered blast hit in the antenna array and cause damage to sensors and communications.

The *Constellation* shot sparks off its hull, unlike anything he could imagine. Gallant shook from the vibrations around him. The temperature in the ship grew so hot that the environmental conditioning system failed. System failures were occurring from every device in the craft.

Looking across the bridge, Gallant saw injured crewmembers.

He was bleeding from a cracked skull.

A Medic asked, "Let me examine you, sir? You're covered in blood."

Making a great effort to keep his voice calm, he said, "A bang on the head. Help the others."

What do I do now?

He had to decide in the blink of an eye.

"Status? What's the ship's status?" As he spoke, as his memory flooded back.

"It's awful, Captain."

Gallant had a momentary impression of his ship like a dying whale floundering in the ocean. He saw the state of the ship as precarious. The Great Ship's weapon had delivered an overpowering blow, but by some miracle, he was still alive.

"XO, what's the damage assessment?"

The XO lit up a console and showed him the silhouette of the ship with red glowing sections throughout. She pointed to the critical areas and the damage control teams that had been dispatched.

Gallant stood swaying on his unsteady feet. He glanced at the console.

Damn! The Great Ship is close.

The enemy was pointing its massive laser

tubes in the direction of the *Constellation*. He opened his mouth to speak but couldn't find the words to express his desire to continue to fight. For the moment, it seemed the Chameleon were content to wait and watch as his ship suffered.

Gallant was shocked by the fear that the Great Ships power wasn't depleted. And it would finish off the *Constellation*. The Great Ship must surely realize that his spacecraft carrier was already crippled. Why would they waste a second shot to administer the coup de grace? It could come at any moment. Why hadn't it happened already? He was so clever in convincing himself that the Chameleon ship could only fire once. He had persuaded himself that that was true. Now he wondered. He listened as if he could hear the next shot. The moaning of the injured bridge crew was loud. Suddenly he was angry with himself. He was wasting time.

The trap!

He had to execute the next move of the trap. He ordered, "Hard to port, come to course 120, azimuth up 10 degrees, at time 1626. All ships, 'execute Blue Bravo.'"

The remaining cruiser and destroyer pivoted on a dime. His maneuvers had gotten them safely outside of the Great Ship's killing region before she shot. Now they needed to turn around and begin firing at the Chameleon ship, hitting her as hard as she had hit them. How far was she? What was she doing? Was there enough time? For minutes of tense anxiety, he waited for his ship to close to their engagement range.

He heard Ryan over the radio, "Starfighters, we have to hit the Great Ship now while its shield strength is depleted!"

"Launch missile!"

Gallant had almost forgotten about his fighters and bombers flying on the perimeter of the battle. Ryan must have ordered them to attack when Gallant gave the "Blue Bravo" signal.

"Thank you, Ryan," Gallant muttered in admonishment to himself for failing to issue the order himself.

The rest of the task force swarmed at the Great Ship and launched missiles. The fighters and bombers were all over it. They concentrated on the spot that Bletchley Circle had identified. Because the Great Ship had expended its main power on the laser, its power level was weak.

The starfighter missiles did serious damage to the Great Ship's reactors. The task force ships added to the enemy's injuries. The task force made repeated attacks, launching missile after missile at the behemoth's vulnerable belly. The giant was hurt. Hurt enough to stagger away with a swarm of starfighters stinging it every kilometer it traveled. The task force had delivered a powerful blow. But despite all their firepower, the Chameleon was able to limp away with several Hawkeyes on its trail.

But back aboard the *Constellation*, things were equally grim. The carrier needed more than damage control for repair; it was gravely wounded and required a major overhaul. In addition, it had lost many starfighters that were on board, which at the time were under maintenance or readiness. The loss of life had to be considered as the most grievous problem to repair.

Gallant didn't want to hear the damage reports and the death toll. It seemed cruel to bring him back to consciousness only to have him face his deepest fears. He felt as if he were in a maze and was just about to turn the final corner to freedom, when *wham*, he's at a dead-end, fallen back upon himself and lost again.

In less than five minutes, fires caused several missile and rocket warheads in the ammunition storage lockers to explode. The ongoing detonations prevented fire suppression efforts during the first critical minutes. The explosions killed fifty. One hundred and forty-one more crew members were killed in other compartments. The conflagration destroyed fighters, blew a hole in the armored flight deck, and sprayed the deck. Burning fuel poured through the hole in the deck into berthing compartments below. Several fully fueled and bomb-laden starfighters caught fire.

Two more explosions ignited shortly after the first, and a fourth blew up seconds after that. Bodies and debris were hurled as far as the bow. An officer recoiled in stunned dismay as burning torches tumbled toward him. Screams stirred him to action. Several men jumped or were blown into space.

Personnel from all over the ship rallied to fight the fires. Damage control teams swarmed over critically damaged areas.

Time went by as workers fell to their task of revitalizing the ship. Electricians, fitters, machinists, welders, and mechanics began performing surgery on the *Constellation*. The XO was coordinating all the activities to keep the pace at maximum. Sparks showered in high arcs, and the rat-tat of mechanical actions went unabated.

Whether the *Constellation* would be fit for action was more a matter of time than not. The deck integrity was being restored, and hatches were being replaced. Structural hull armor sheets were being moved into position. The clock was running faster to get after the enemy.

The game wasn't over.

CHAPTER 18

Pivot

Gallant's in-basket was flooded. From every corner of the ship, urgent action messages demanded his attention. A line of officers stood outside his stateroom, waiting to update him of the sad condition of his ship and crew.

The head of the medical department was first.

"The death count has grown since yesterday," said the doctor grimly. He handed Gallant an updated list.

Gallant pictured the face of each person.

The doctor said, "Unfortunately, two medical centers were destroyed, along with many rejuvenation tanks. We had to requisition medical supplies from other ships."

Gallant asked, "Is the remaining equipment adequate?"

The doctor brightened. "Yes, sir. The prognosis for the rest of the injured is good. I don't think we'll lose any more."

The physician showed him an AI analysis of

the treatment plan.

"Thank you, Doctor."

After the doctor left, the ship's engineer was next to enter.

Commander Harris said, "A massive repair effort is underway. The integrity of the hull is our immediate priority. Once we get the holes patched, we'll rebuild or replace essential equipment."

"I want the flight deck operational as soon as possible."

"Aye aye, sir," said Harris. "The engine room should follow."

"Agreed."

Harris said, "The weapon systems will be tough and slow, I'm afraid. The officers and crew are keeping everything moving with only occasional oversight from me."

Gallant gave him a weak smile.

"Here are my recommendations for repairing salvageable equipment," said Harris, "along with my suggestions for scraping replacements parts from other ships."

He handed the tablet to Gallant.

Harris said, "The reactors are in sad shape. Some had core melting. One is a total write-off. I'm afraid we won't be seeing anything over fifty percent acceleration any time soon. The ship's hull includes several breaches, which are currently isolated but will need significant patching until we get back to Sol. The stealth technology was not significantly damaged, but several support systems were set on fire, and they must be replaced."

"What about personnel?" asked Gallant.

Numerous members of the crew suffered radiation burns or fire injuries. We have enough rates to stand watch and battle stations once sickbay returns those that are able."

Harris said, "We are about fifty percent operational now, and I guess we will be eighty percent in a few days."

"That will have to do until we get to a shipyard," said Gallant shaking his head.

Harris updated Gallant's tablet with detailed tables and schedules of repair plans.

Gallant said, "Run this list past the XO. She's working on the personnel roster for each rating."

"Aye aye, sir."

They were interrupted by squawking from the intercom, "Captain to the bridge! Captain to the bridge!"

Gallant's appearance on the bridge was greeted with the OOD saying, "A scout drone has identified a close contact."

Gallant said, "Sound general quarters. Ready the CSP to intercept. Move the standby CSP into launch position."

The klaxon blasted.

CLANG! CLANG! CLANG!

There was a flurry of activity and many anxious faces over the next few minutes.

Finally, a follow-up report identified the contact as a meteorite.

The intercom blared, "Resume the normal watch."

The OOD relaxed general quarters, and the rest of the morning watch was uneventful.

Gallant settled into his command chair and asked, "XO, give me an accounting of our losses."

Fletcher reported, "We lost the *Invincible*, and destroyers *Ellis*, *Staverton*, *Dewey*, and *Conway*. Cruisers *Marlborough* and *Wilmot* are write-offs, Skipper."

She shook her head, "I recommend that we send them to Davey Jones' Locker."

"Roger that."

"Aye aye, sir. I'll make arrangements."

"Damaged ships?" he asked.

"Cruiser *Vincennes* was walloped."

"Damn."

She added, "The remaining destroyers suffered varying degrees of damage. I'm afraid repairs will be extensive. I'll send a list to your inbox."

Gallant asked, "What's the latest reconnaissance report."

"Hawkeye-11 reported that they followed the retreating Great Ship. It wasn't cloaked. It took refuge in a cluster of several one hundred-kilometer sized asteroids. The location of its cubbyhole is plotted on your data file. It looks like they're preparing to do extensive repairs. Work has started on missile batteries on the neighboring asteroids."

Gallant examined the construction underway

for the Great Ship's protection. The fortified missile batteries were designed as forts A, B, C, and D.

"XO, we have to strike quick. We have an opportunity while the Great Ship remains vulnerable. We might not get another chance."

"You're right, sir."

"I'll need the Marines."

Gallant drew up a daring plan. He intended to use speed, stealth, and surprise to deliver a devastating blow—just the sort of joint operation that his starfighters and Marines would be eager to execute. But first, he had to regroup his forces. He was proud of the task force's strength except for the one thing that mattered most, its comparison to his enemy.

He said, "OOD, transmit this order to Major Steward on Charlie."

> From: Commander Task Force 34
> To: Major James Steward
> Subj: Deployment
> Ref: (a) Comm Order UP 034404 (b) Space Combat Mission Directive
> 1. Under Reference (a) Major James Steward is directed to embark the 1st Marine Raider Battalion on assigned transport.
> 2. The Battalion is to travel under escort to the asteroid field and rendezvous with Task Force 34
> 3. When directed, 1st Marine Raider Battalion will undertake an assault on for-

tified asteroid missile batteries as per the attached Reference (b).
4. Report to task force no later than Monday, Sept 16th, 0800 hours.

Henry Gallant
Captain Henry Gallant
Commander, Task Force 34

The OOD reported, "Message to Major Steward has been sent, sir."

"Very well," said Gallant.

Next, Gallant arranged to regroup Task Force 34. He ordered the OOD, "Transmit this order to the rest of the task force."

From: Commander Task Force 34
To: Captain Jackson, Task Force 34.1
   Captain Hernandez, Task Force 34.2
   Captain Chu Task Force 34.3
Subj: Reform Task Force 34
Ref: (a) Comm Order UP 034405 (b) Task Force Operations Order

1. Under Reference (a) the addressees shall rendezvous with Task Force 34.4
2. Task Force 34.1 will escort the 1st Marine Raider Battalion traveling in transports.
3. Rendezvous no later than Monday, Sept 16th, 0800 hours.

Henry Gallant
Captain Henry Gallant
Commander, Task Force 34

Over the next week, the various units converged. Soon *Constellation* sailed alongside the *Courageous*, the *Indefatigable*, and the *Inflexible*. Nearby, several troop transport vessels carried the Marines. They were surrounded by escorts. A bare minimum of cruisers and destroyers had been left behind for convoy duty.

Gallant drew a deep breath of pride as Task Force 34 sailed toward the Great Ship's hidey-hole.

CHAPTER 19

Strike 1

The *Constellation* and *Courageous* roiled with preparations for an attack on the Great Ship. As far as the pilots were concerned, the sooner the attack got started, the better. They had enough trouble without costly delays to their timetable.

As wing commander, Lieutenant Rob Ryan felt the weight of responsibility as the final minutes ticked away. Anxiety stretched over every inch of his scarred face. Scars are a stark reminder that combat has consequences. He absentmindedly rubbed the jagged red creases.

Why worry?

This was no different from a score of other missions he'd flown. It was practically routine.

He felt a tap on his shoulder and turned to find his flight chief trying to make himself heard over the flight deck noise.

"Lucky 7 is humming perfectly and ready for whatever you need, sir."

"Thanks, Chief."

Ryan reached up and grabbed the handhold of his bad-ass Viper. He sprang the cockpit latch and flopped into the starfighter's seat. Inserting his breathing hose, he turned to attach his neural net and bring the AI to life. He scanned his AI computer and flipped through the navigation chart and targeting assignment. He pressed buttons and flipped switches until finally, his checklist was complete. Strapping in, he tapped the controls impatiently.

Surrounding the fighter was a flight crew pulling out replenishment hoses and cable connections. One after another, the fighters lined up into their launch position. Though the flight deck was crowded at the moment, Ryan could envision when soon hundreds of square meters would become an empty metal deck.

The crew chief gave him a thumbs up, rapped twice on the cockpit, and then jumped out of the way. The rest of the flight crew scrambled to their sheltered positions as Ryan started the engine. It roared and bellowed as the temperature and pressure behind the craft changed radically.

The fighter was towed into launch position, and the launch officer said, "Condition green for catapult one. All flight crews take ready positions."

Ryan's space wing consisted of Viper Is, Viper IIs, and Hawkeye spaceships.

The F-789 Viper I was a sleek, elegant fighter capable of accelerating to 0.3 C in less than six hours. Its optimal attack speed was 0.2 C. It had life support for seven days. It sported a pulsed laser cannon capable of punching through titanium armor. The Mongoose X anti-missile missile had its own ECM and was an effective counter to most enemy missiles. The Vulture VI was a heavy weapon missile used against ships and fortifications.

The F-789a Viper II was a fighter-bomber, which was essentially a Viper I fighter with an externally mounted heavy missile rack. The rack could carry the huge Goliath super antimatter missile.

And the starfighter fleet couldn't be complete without the Hawkeye's reconnaissance. Its thirty-day life support, long-range sensors, and AI neural data-lined computers made it an indispensable forward command asset. It carried an extra payload of ECM gear for jamming, decoys, and intercepting communication signals. With a crew of three, it was four times the size of a Viper.

The flight deck's hanger doors opened, exposing the fighters to the cold vacuum of space.

Ryan reported to the flight operations officer, "Ready to launch."

A moment later, the flight officer started the launch countdown. Ten seconds later, the words "launch starfighters!" were given.

Ryan revved his engine as Lucky 7 was catapulted from the *Constellation* like a slingshot shooting a stone.

Forty-eight fighters and seventy-two bombers from the two carriers took their station in formation. Six Hawkeyes went ahead. The space wing set off to bomb the Great Ship.

The mission got off to a ragged start as a fighter reported an engine issue and was forced to return to the *Courageous*.

Ryan was upset because this reflected poorly on his preparation for the mission. He ordered a fighter to fill in the open slot in the formation.

The flight chart showed a trajectory through the asteroid field with many twists and turns. He worried as the formation made the necessary maneuvers and some pilots were slow or sloppy. His temper flared when he saw that Joe Flannery was already out of position.

"Bear, you're veering to port," he said.

"Roger."

Samuel Rhodes was falling behind, as well.

"Dusty, snap it up."

"Roger."

It took two hours to reach the "Beast," Ryan's nickname for the Great Ship. The Hawkeyes kept the Great Ship under long-distance surveillance.

Ten light-minutes out, Ryan ordered the Hawkeyes to launch twenty recon drones. Recon drones were small, fast, stealthy projectiles good for short sneaky activities. The drones collected vital information about the defenses.

The initial report identified a minefield and plotted thousands that were strewn in their path. They were deadly. The volume and location of their placement meant business.

Mines were only the first obstacle the starfighters faced. Follow-up reconnaissance showed missile batteries deployed among the asteroids around the Great Ship.

The drones linked their data-feed to Hawkeye-1 and provided essential information. The Hawkeye's computer processed the raw data and focused on critical locations.

Ryan read the Hawkeye report on his console. At five light-minutes out, he ordered, "Hawkeye-1 begin ECM."

"Roger that," snapped Kelsey. She ordered the other Hawkeyes to launch decoys and begin jamming the enemy sensors. She used her neural net command link to distribute targeting plots on the mines and missile batteries.

Three light minutes out, Ryan ordered the *Courageous* fighters to take their attack position. As Squadron 7 separated and swung toward the minefield, the enemy forts launched a barrage of missiles. The Hawkeyes jammed the missiles' sensors and fired a swarm of Mongoose missiles. Decoys were released that proved helpful in confusing the incoming missiles.

A flanking fighter exploded for no apparent reason. Ryan didn't know the minefield extended that far in front of them. Now he did. It was a costly lesson.

Ryan ordered, "Squadron 7, blow a hole in that minefield."

A minute later, the Antz began their march through the minefield. The Antz antimine plasma blasts did their job. They ignited rows of mines that sympathetically exploded, producing a domino effect. The flashes highlighted a glaring hole through the field.

"Outstanding," said Ryan. "Now, if everything goes smoothly, we're in the clear."

Two light-minutes out, *Constellation's* Squadron 6 flew through the minefield hole.

The defensive forts meant that the fighters would be exposed as they came in. It was a risky environment. Ryan was surprised at the volume of missile defense being thrown up around the Beast.

The forts opened with a withering missile fire. Missile salvos ripped through the fighters.

"Six unknowns, inboard," said one pilot.

"Wideband emissions," said another pilot.

"More bogeys to port."

Ryan ordered, "Take evasive action."

Several fighters diverted and broke off. The sizzling fire followed them.

As the pilots struggled, Ryan ordered Vultures launched at the missile forts. He couldn't expect to destroy those well-defended positions, but he hoped to suppress their fire.

The fighters continued their attack on the forts. The fighters sliced past the outer missile batteries only to resort to evasive maneuvers that stifled their progress. They did considerable damage but couldn't penetrate close enough to knock them out.

Ryan's Viper had great acceleration and a small turning radius, which helped him dodge the missiles. But his expertise wasn't shared by many other pilots. It was like a body blow when he witnessed several fighters take hits and call for help. A couple of escape pods burst free.

As the bombers closed in on their target, Ryan scanned the battlespace. He worked to coordinate the squadrons. Time seemed to slow as he snapped out orders for assignment.

"Squadron 7, attack the sunward forts."

He admonished Glenn Holman, who was flying erratically.

An energy missile signature lit up Ryan's console.

He yelled, "Incoming!"

A volley of mic clicks sounded over tac1, acknowledging.

He launched a Mongoose and watched the enemy missile die in a fireball.

Right behind the fighters, bomber Squadrons 8 and 9 arrived and began their run.

"Lucky. Request permission to attack target," said Lorelei.

"Permission granted, Flame."

Considering the size of the strike, Ryan hoped the bombers' attack would be devastating.

The Great Ship's radar spotted the incoming attack and threw up a horrific point defense flak. It included missiles, lasers, projectile, and plasma fire. At maximum range, she looked braced for the ordeal.

The starfighters launched an anti-missile barrage. They released decoys and began jamming signals.

But Lorelei's bomber group had trouble. The bomber squadrons headed into a blistering barrage as the nearby forts spit out a flurry of missiles. It was close quarters, and despite the bombers' evasive maneuvers, they took losses.

Disregarding the fortress fire, Lorelei ordered the bombers to close on the target. The Great Ship was tucked away in a dense asteroid cluster between several huge rocky bodies. The missile batteries protected the best approach. Attacking bombers had to pass close to the fortification.

Although the interlocking missile batteries were a powerful barrier, some well-aimed Mongoose scored.

"Fire missiles!" ordered Lorelei. Her bomber twitched as each Goliath was ejected.

"Birds away!" came the response from the squadrons.

The Goliath antimatter warhead exploded matter and antimatter in a fraction of a second. It annihilated so completely that, except for a flash of visible light, only x-rays and gamma rays remained.

The bombers launched their weapons, but the Great Ship's shield was so formidable that it caused the missiles to explode prematurely, far from the ship's titanium hull. This dispersed the weapon's fireball before it could achieve maximum damage.

One ship disintegrated, then one bomber after another was hit. More starfighters were lost over the next few minutes as they completed their bombing runs.

It was time to head back to the barn.

Despite the furious defense, the starfighters came remarkably close to scoring some potent hits. In the end, the sacrifices were in vain. The Great Ship sustained no serious damage. The forts had done their job.

The pilots were sullen for the entire two-hour flight back to the carriers.

On returning to the *Constellation*, Ryan made a poor approach to the flight deck. The instant his fighter touched down, the fighter careened to one side and skidded from a sloppy landing. He was relieved that no serious damage was done to his craft, but he was embarrassed as he went to the ready room.

Ryan was not pleased with the day's effort and made that clear at the debriefing. The foray had been costly with little return—a desperate venture gone awry. A fair criticism was that they hadn't prepared enough and lacked vital intelligence on the forts. But they did learn a lot that would prove useful in the future. He recommended a second strike.

The game isn't over.

CHAPTER 20

Fallout

Gallant was surprised that a delegation of civilian captains made the journey to the asteroid belt to meet with him. Task Force 34 was in the middle of a battle against the Great Ship. He didn't have time for them. They persisted until he relented and agreed to host them aboard the *Constellation*.

"What's so important it can't wait until this battle's resolution?" demanded Gallant of the collection of captains standing bunched together in his stateroom.

Captain Daux spoke first. He pointed to Gallant and stammered, "You've taken away our convoy escorts."

"I have reformed Task Force 34 to fight the enemy. Two cruisers and two squadrons of destroyers remain as convoy escorts. That is all I can spare. It should be enough to keep the Titan raiders at bay."

"No. No, it isn't enough," said NNR manager, Grover Miller.

"You're here as well, Mister Miller?" asked Gallant.

"Of course. This issue is at the heart of the NNR business. You will imperil our productivity."

Gallant scanned the room, and his eyes landed on the balding head of the mining consortium leader. "What is your opinion, Captain Wells?"

"Oh, I understand that striking the enemy improves our fortunes in the long term. It's the short term we've come to see you about."

"I've scheduled the next convoy to proceed with the only available escorts I can spare," said Gallant. "However, if you are fearful, we can delay convoys until the Great Ship is defeated."

Though the Chameleon ship had been damaged, it retained great destructive capability. The Hawkeyes managed to follow the ship to its position in the asteroids where it appeared to be undergoing repairs. Gallant's concern remained as great as ever. He mulled over the possibilities of acting against the ship while continuing to protect the convoys.

The room reverberated with grumbling.

"Who knows when that will be?" said one captain.

"We'll go broke by then," said another.

"That's no solution," said a captain shaking his head.

Captain Wells said, "*Star Rover* has to keep moving and making money."

"If you're successful, it would be a welcome psychological boost as well as a material victory for all of us," said Miller. "But we can't count on that."

"The whole system of convoys is unsound," concluded Captain Daux.

The discussion lingered for nearly an hour before Gallant agreed to add one additional destroyer squadron to the convoys' defense.

Wearing a mask of sincerity on his face, Wells said, "Thank you, Captain Gallant."

As the others filed out of the stateroom, Miller and Wells remained behind.

Wells offered his hand and clasped Gallant's hand firmly. "I want to discuss a thorny problem only you can resolve. The issue is one of accounting. The good news is that you're in the best position to solve it. I won't sugar-coat it. The odds are there will be political fallout. Maybe considerable."

"Please explain."

Miller said, "First, did you know that Governor Stein sent a message to Earth requesting that you be replaced."

Gallant didn't know, but he wasn't surprised. He leaned forward but remained silent.

Wells said, "Unfortunately, Stein hasn't listened to our advice. The governor is under pressure to deliver material, and he is willing to run the high risk. His attitude was ungracious, and uncooperative. To be frank, Stein has his own agenda, and I, and the other mining operators, need your help."

"What can I do?"

"We are conducting a financial audit of NNR and the entire mining operation. We need your authority to give it teeth."

"An audit?" asked Gallant.

"Yes. We suspect an accounting shortfall—irregularities, fraud—perhaps embezzlement. Millions of tons of minerals have disappeared and are unaccounted for."

"Those are serious accusations. Whom do you suspect?"

"I'm not naming names. Not yet. That's why the audit is necessary. And why we need the backing of the Navy."

Gallant said, "Conduct your audit and submit your findings to the task force. If we can substantiate them, the Navy will take appropriate action."

CHAPTER 21

Jetpack

Major James Steward squeezed into the cramped quarters of the transport ship. The troop transport was not his favorite mode of travel. It was a five-day journey from Charlie to the rally point at the edge of the asteroid belt. He expected to be uncomfortable every minute of that. Despite his unpleasant situation, he kept himself fit by using a small exercise room that allowed him to work out once a day. There was a strict rotation cycle, so he had to be on time. Besides exercise, there was little else to do. But the in-ship training program was extensive, and he looked forward to them to break the boredom.

Sergeant Mike McCauley scheduled physical fitness exercises in the morning and jetpack training in the afternoons. While traveling through space at a constant velocity, the Marines were able to conduct jetpack ops around the transport. The jetpacks were fun at first but maneuvering in space as part of a group was demanding.

Steward led a squad in jetpacks for a spin around the ship. Training for the real thing to come meant teamwork. The suit named the Daedalus Mark 77, used six tiny jet engines — two mounted on the wearer's back, with an additional two mounted on each arm—which allows a Marine to fly through space in a controlled flight. The Marines jetted back and forth, aided by a helmet equipped with a heads-up display that provided flight data and fuel usage. It gave military soldiers considerable speed and freedom of movement. The suits were armored and carried small arms weapons.

Some operational kinks needed to be worked out in training. The suit microturbines were for vertical takeoffs and landings, as well as level flight. Two of these turbines were situated together with the main fuel tanks, an assembly that the user wore like a backpack. The flier then had two more turbines in mounts on each forearm for lateral control. Improvements to the design were constantly being considered.

McCauley didn't know what the Marines would be thrown into, but he wanted to be prepared for any possibility. He set up his training plan accordingly. At first, the Marines easily traversed McCauley's extemporized obstacle course. Soon they found him expanding the course, and things became harder.

He hoped the training would be enough.

CHAPTER 22

Strike 2

The ejection thrust hit Lieutenant Rob Ryan like a hammer, throwing him back against the seat, forcing the air out of his lungs. Shaking off the effects, he throttled his engine to match the slingshot's thrust as the Viper cleared the launch bay and sailed into space. The g's climbed as the ship gathered momentum and speed. The stars on his scope rotated in his view, and he glanced at the task force around him. He turned to the starboard to bring his ship on course and set the peg position for the formation. The ship vibrated and shook until he settled on a steady path.

    He waited until the rest of the squadrons took station. The preflight briefing had detailed the attack plan. It followed standard procedures for coordinating the fighters and bombers for a strike. It required precision timing and unswerving dedication to teamwork. The flight would break into multiple arms, directing the attack to strike the target at once by dividing the enemy defense. This offered the best opportunity for a kill. But it severely restricted improvisation.

The Great Ship was out there, and the task force's existence depended on the starfighters dealing it a fatal blow. The latest Hawkeye reports stated that the ship was nearly operational. An epic battle was in the offering. They couldn't fail again.

The attack consisted of forty-eight bombers carrying the new Goliath warhead. The Goliath had a fusion primary and antimatter secondary warhead capable of penetrating the toughest titanium hull—if it exploded on contact. The problem was getting close enough to get the warhead through the ship's shield. Thirty-six fighters served as escorts.

"I hope this goes better than before," said Bear.

"Yeah, anything different would be better than the last time," said Werewolf.

The reports from the recon drones showed no new enemy movement. Would the Great Ship start erect new defenses before the attack was thrown in? Ryan hoped not. They were beginning to think the Great Ship was an invulnerable monster. It was the pride of the Chameleon.

For now, he was the hunter, and the Great Ship was his prey. He didn't expect that would remain for long.

They were approaching the target. Ryan ordered his ships to decelerate. Nothing was to be gained by an early appearance at the enemy's stronghold.

The starfighters were several million kilometers from the Great Ship when Ryan ordered, "GO! GO!"

The starfighters approached the asteroids and broke through the minefield. The squadrons worked together to reach the launch point.

As the first wave approached, the Chameleon's warning system alerted them. The fighters had not achieved surprise, but it took several minutes for the Great Ship's batteries to be manned.

One starfighter was lost immediately.

The fighters concentrated their fire on the fortification around the Great Ship. But they were not getting enough weapons on target.

Ryan said, "I thought there was a back door through the asteroid forts. But they've put up a new battery."

"This is déjà vu," said Bear.

"I agree. We're in for it," said Werewolf.

"If anything. It's worse," said Dusty.

Ryan's fighters targeted the forts while Lorelei's Viper led the bombers. The bombers arrived over their target minutes later and were met by the full fury of the defense.

For the bomber pilots of the *Constellation* and *Courageous*, the mission got complicated. They faced the defenses of battle stations and many missile batteries. Plasma guns and missiles raced skyward. So many things happened at once. They could have been shot out of space by the Beast.

Despite the missile batteries, only six bombers had been shot down. Then another bomber was lost. More followed in quick succession.

Lorelei prepared to launch the first set of missiles from the external racks.

She ordered, "Fire!"

She heard, "Missiles away!"

Bomber Squadrons 8 and 9 sent their Goliath missiles at the Great Ship.

They hoped to whack the enemy, but the result was a flop.

Before Ryan could swallow the bitter taste of disappointment, he was shaken by a near-miss explosion. He moved farther from the dense enemy fire. A few minutes later, his ship received a plasma hit to the engine. He hit the fire suppressant switch and flapped at the cockpit flames with his bare hands.

With his heart pounding, he ordered, "Break contact!"

CHAPTER 23

Ghost Signal

Kate met with Logan each morning to plan the day's activities. They shared time examining artifacts but often spent time individually in the virtual world. Sometimes they revisited the VR several times a day. At first, Kate tried to be concise and restrained. To her surprise, Logan always responded quickly to every suggestion. Usually, it was a single, terse sentence. But, over time, his replies grew longer. Their relationship grew and started to include personal details. Whenever he arrived at the lab, she dropped what she was doing to work together. Before long, they were talking for hours, and their conversations grew long and rambling. She found him intriguing. They had lots in common, and she seemed to get his jokes, which was a big plus. By this method, their thinking began to coalesce.

The Bletchley Circle team had expanded to include techs from the *Constellation* and SIA techs working in the bunker. Kate was a natural leader and made all the work assignments, including Logan's.

He cheerfully followed her instructions. She requisitioned computer equipment from every corner of the planet. She even managed to get the *Constellation* to allow her samples of missile parts on the theory that Bletchley might have to interface with them at some point. Their offices were crammed with computer gear of every description, all yammering at once.

Kate swiped a lock of hair out of her eyes as she typed code into her virtual reality program, line by line. The AI was constantly interfering by overwriting her efforts with syntax corrections. She didn't mind that so much, but when it started showing bubbles of suggested code on her display, she erupted.

"Code assist, stop!"

She hated the interference from a dumb machine trying to be smarter than she was. Her IQ was over 200, and though the AI could beat her at chess, it couldn't come close to programming as well as she could.

The click and clatter of the dozen other programmers in the laboratory didn't disturb her. She was lost in concentration.

At first, Logan only shared professional research and theories. But after a while, he no longer worried about divulging personal information to her. They made plans for exploring the virtual reality world together and enjoyed the adventure. He found that Kate was quite different from normal people.

"We've been over this a hundred times," said Logan, discouraged after repeated failures. "There's nothing here. We've hit a brick wall."

"Then we will retrench," she said. "Go bigger. Expand our search. Expand our thinking."

"Where do we look? We've already looked everywhere. There's nothing left to explore," Logan argued.

"You're wrong. There's always *one* more."

"One more, what?"

"Haven't you ever had a jar of mixed nuts? You pick out your favorites first, of course."

"Of course," sneered Logan.

"But when you think there are none of your favorites left, you give it a shake," said Kate.

"So."

"There's always one more. One hidden gem left among the rejects. You work to scavenge them, but you keep looking because there is always one. Every time you think you're done another pops up."

"So?"

"So, there will be one more place for us to look. We just have to find it."

Kate renewed her efforts in the virtual reality world of the Great Ship. She narrowed her attention to the AI system controlling the shield. To her dismay, she began hearing whispers. They were coming from inside the virtual reality world. It frightened her at first, but after a while, she got an idea.

She spent a solitary evening doing research until she was flabbergasted. She wandered to the edge of the virtual world and considered a forbidden possibility. The Chameleon might have devised a mental trap to protect their precious shield technology. Perhaps there was a software tool hidden in their AI that might be running, unknown to her in her virtual world. Kate's mind recoiled at the thought of a Chameleon mind trap.

She gasped, "The AI might be trying to gain control of my mind in some elaborate ambush." She put her hands on her neural net skullcap when a thought popped into her mind.

What kind of person runs away when she is about to solve her greatest puzzle?

"Did I think that?" asked Kate. "Or was that planted by an AI trap?"

The thought recurred—*What kind of person runs away when she is about to solve her greatest puzzle?*

"A person who doesn't want to lose her mind," said Kate. "I will never let them take me!"

She pulled the neural net skullcap off her head, breaking contact with the virtual world. She spent a few minutes pondering what had happened.

Logan was in the laboratory examining an artifact. But she decided she should do more investigating before telling him. She underwent a brain scan but found nothing dangerous. Going back into the virtual world environment, she adjusted the settings. With a twist of the dial, she reproduced the whispering. Pleased with herself, she was in control of the situation this time.

Her first step was to ensure that the whispering wasn't part of a Chameleon mind trap. An idea began to form. She needed to bootstrap the idea and live long enough to tell Logan. She tested it. She was beginning to understand what the whispering meant.

Leaving the virtual reality world, she pulled Logan aside, away from the techs.

"I heard whispering," she stammered.

"Don't start that again," Logan said, frowning. "It's just the harsh wind outside the bunker."

"I'm not talking about the howling from outside."

"What then?"

She said, "I heard whispering... like a *ghost*!"

"Don't go all supernatural on me," said Logan. He was losing patience with her fanciful imaginings. "There aren't any ghosts trying to contact you."

"I don't mean a *ghost* ghost."

"Huh?"

"I mean a ghost signal."

"So, tell me all about what's overstimulated your curiosity this time."

"I was working in the virtual world on the AI controls for the shield. As I adjusted the shield frequency settings, I heard whispering."

He grunted.

"There was a pattern to the noise." She smacked him on the shoulder. "At first, I thought I might have stumbled across an elaborate AI mind trap set by the Chameleon."

"What!"

"Relax. It wasn't that."

"What then?"

"I figured it out! It's a signal inside a signal."

"We're not codebreakers. We can't decrypt Chameleon communications," said Logan

"No. It wasn't communication. It wasn't a code."

Logan said, "Okay, enlighten me."

She sighed. "I built the virtual world simulation to realistically mimic characteristics of the Chameleon ship. I had lots of data, and I created a good facsimile of their technology. It mirrors the performance and processes of the actual Great Ship protective shield."

"And I've told you repeatedly that you did a great job."

"Thanks. I think the VR captures the wave frequencies of the shield device. The whispering I hear when I work on it is an aftereffect of that."

"An aftereffect of the shield signal itself?"

"Yes. It's a ghost signal that quantum tunnels through the shield defense. It's formed when the operational waves interfere with each other."

"So, what good is that?"

"Don't you see? We can use the frequency of the ghost signal to penetrate the ship's shield. Missiles would be invisible to the shield and wouldn't detonate until they hit the hull."

"Oh, I see. This is a guide frequency for penetrating the shield. We could build microprocessors that could follow the ghost signal. Once we put the microprocessors into our missiles, the Great Ship will be doomed."

He smacked his hands together. "You've done

it. You've found the third key. Congratulations!" said Logan joyfully, giving her a hug.

Kate looked surprised at his reaction but couldn't hide her pleasure.

Logan called the techs around and told them the news. He immediately set them to work building microprocessors to his specification.

CHAPTER 24

Strike 3

Weak and feverish, Ryan struggled into his uniform. He left sickbay before fully recovering from his combat wounds. But more than physical pain, he was exhausted. Worry and traumatic shock had left him numb. He was going through the motions and he could sense his breaking point was coming.

As the space wing prepared for another attack, the fleet's mood was far less confident than a few days earlier. Ryan argued with the CIC officer about the danger of the latest intelligence assessment. His main concern was the new fortification upgrades around the Great Ship. After reviewing the scouting data, Ryan made some rapid calculations. Examining the missile battery holograph and target assessment, he considered taking an alternate flight path.

Lieutenant Jacobs assured him that the CIC analysis concluded that he need not worry.

This sequence of events led Ryan to the fateful conclusion that things were spinning out of control.

He faced an appalling choice between two unpalatable options. Either way, many would die, possibly with little benefit.

He chose the alternate flight path. He did not spell out the reasons to redirect the mission course. The briefing was over quickly, and none of the pilots objected. Their priorities were set. The starfighters were given a final onceover by the crew chiefs—all weapons, sensors and communication gear checked out.

An hour later, the speakers blared—calling the flight crews to move the starfighters into launch position. Bellowing motors pulled spacecraft along the runways from their hangers to their catapults.

Ryan welcomed the sound of engines singing in his ears. He passed Lorelei at the flight deck hatch.

"How are you?" she asked.

"I'm sorry to be absent so long," he said. "The rejuvenation chamber treatment was extensive."

"I'm sorry to hear that. Are you really able to fly?"

He shrugged. "I'm better than before."

The glint in his eyes hinted that he was more ill than he was confessing. He asked her about the health of several of her pilots.

"They're already on the flight line," said Lorelei. Then with a frown, she added, "You should let your wingman lead the attack. You need more rest."

"I've got a job to do," said Ryan shaking his head. "So, do you. You'd better get to your fighter."

He pushed passed her and tried to open the

hatch into the next compartment. In his weakened state, he could barely crack it open. Fearing Lorelei would guess how fragile he was, he threw himself against the hatch to force it free. He staggered through and almost collapsed on the other side.

She said, "Rob, you're too weak to go on this mission. Let alone lead it."

He displayed a remarkable strength of mind over matter and pulled himself erect.

"I'm able to go, and I'm going. You can't stop me."

He pressed past her and climbed aboard his Viper.

The attack did not go well.

The thirty-four bombers and twenty-two fighters faced a horrific rate of missile, plasma, and projectile fire. The missile batteries poking from the surrounding asteroids were effectively positioned. They sent scores of missiles at the bombers. The Great Ship's point-defense acquitted itself well, parrying the blows of the bombers. The Beast expended tons of rounds from her main projectile defenses. The Chameleon defense drove the bombers away without allowing any critical hits.

One Goliath bomb did penetrate the upper armor deck, but its fuse was damaged, and it did not detonate. A second Goliath did explode against the hull but only caused minor damage on the armor.

The attack left few injuries to the Chameleon but gaping holes in the starfighters. Many fighters and bombers were shot down. Numerous more were damaged.

Ryan wanted to punch the enemy in the gut, but the result was a jab to the nose. He radioed, "There is an urgent need for another attack."

CHAPTER 25

Debrief

Ryan led the returning starfighters back to the *Constellation*. They landed on the flight deck, one after another.

The flight chief counted until he shook his head soberly, "Ten fewer have returned than left."

One member of the flight crew carried a wound man from his fighter. He shouted, "I need a medic. Quick!"

Several men and women ran to his side.

A responding medic shook his head sadly. "He's had it."

The XO stood on the flight deck searching through the returning pilots. She found Ryan and asked, "Where's Joe Mallory?"

"He didn't make it," said Ryan. "A projectile barrage shattered his fighter while he was making a pass at a missile battery."

They were forced to move to one side as another injured pilot was carried passed them.

Fletcher felt a stab of sympathy. "I guess you

don't feel much like talking."

"That's okay. I'll be fine." Ryan turned and led the pilots to the debriefing room. He welcomed the sight of his 'Squadron 6 Mascot' coffee mug on the table. It was full of hot, steaming coffee. He grasped it in two hands and drank a great gulp. The hot liquid burned his throat as it went down. He didn't mind. It was what he needed. His tight, knotted muscles tried to relax but the aftershock of the battle was still coursing through his system.

Gallant, the XO, and several CIC intelligence officers made up the debriefing team. They sat in front of a long table. The many chairs on the other side were filled with pilots in various states of disarray.

Gallant and the XO listened as the interrogations began.

One CIC officer asked, "What was the count?"

Ryan said, "We lost four in Squadron 6. Six are missing from Squadron 8. I don't have a count from *Courageous*, yet."

The CIC officer glanced at Gallant who was listening off to one side.

Gallant clicked on his communicator to the OOD. He ordered, "Send SAR teams to look for survivors. Turn the homing beacon to the maximum." Then he returned his attention to the debriefing.

The XO place her hand on Ryan's shoulder and said, "Take us through the mission."

Ryan said, "We began on time at 06:00. One ship turned back with engine trouble. Other than that, we had an uneventful passage. It took two hours and seven minutes to get to the target. Once we reached the fortified missile batteries, things got bad. We got hit pretty hard on the first pass. That's when Joe got it."

The XO nodded.

"The action continued, and we lost several more. Then the bombers made their run. They got hit just as bad by the batteries. Many of their ships were pretty shot up. I'm afraid we didn't get many hits through the shield, and most of those didn't do much damage."

"What's your assessment of the current state of the Great Ship?" asked the CIC officer.

Ryan looked crescent fallen. "We're going to need another strike."

"What's the problem?" asked Gallant. "I need an answer to understand how another strike will be any different."

Ryan said, "The second group was three minutes late over the target. That cost us. The forts were able to concentrate their fire on the first group."

The XO said, "Each group leader bears part of that blame, but you're the wing commander. It's your job to take mitigating action when necessary."

Ryan grimaced.

The CIC officer asked, "Were there other problems you could identify?"

Ryan said, "There are no perfect plans. We used an alternate navigation route through the asteroids. I hoped it would offer us better cover."

CIC officer, Lieutenant Jacobs, asked, "Did it?"

"Not much. Not enough. It was bad luck."

The drily reported facts were not comforting.

"What other problems did you encounter?" asked Jacobs.

Ryan growled, "I'll tell you the problem. You keep sending us back into that meat grinder without a chance of success. We keep taking losses without results. If our luck doesn't change, we're going to keep losing men and machines."

Standing up, Gallant towered over Ryan. "You talk a lot about luck. You even named your Viper, 'Lucky 7.' I don't believe in luck. I believe you make your own luck. There's always a reason for failure."

Ryan hung his head.

Gallant sat back down and spoke quietly, "In the past, I rated you pretty high. The situation is we must keep at this mission until the job is done. There is no other alternative. You've got to be tough enough to see it through."

"I don't know how to do that," muttered Ryan, averting his gaze.

"You've been through a lot," said Gallant. "You've led a lot of missions. Perhaps you're feeling sorry for yourself."

Shaking his head, Ryan said, "That's not true."

"If you're as hot as you've claimed to be, prove it," said Fletcher.

Ryan grimaced.

"If you feel you're not up to the task any longer," said Gallant, "I'll relieve you as wing commander."

Ryan felt as if a bucket of cold water had been thrown into his face. He opened his mouth and closed it. Then he said, "No, sir. That's not necessary." Instantly, he reconsidered his response—let someone else deal with the trouble. But he said, "Give me another chance, sir."

Gallant took a minute to collect his thoughts. "I'm not going to pass the buck to a new commander. You're going to have to live up to your decision to stay. If a man like you can't cut it, we've had it."

Ryan said, "I can get it done."

After the debriefing, Gallant remained in the room with Fletcher.

Fletcher said, "Besides the normal stress of flying dangerous missions, these pilots have suffered personal loss. Many of their friends have died. And many of them have been injured and returned to duty." She uttered the words in her classic understated manner. Her face remained impassive.

"We can't stop until the job is done," said Gallant.

"The blame for failure doesn't rest with the wing commander or the pilots," said Fletcher, who was not given to exaggeration. "They needed something to make a difference. And it's up to us to provide it or change the mission."

"We have a responsibility."

"The atmosphere aboard the *Constellation* has turned gloomy. Indeed, the disappointment is palpable. The CIC planners were confused about what they could do to make a difference in another attack. They must reorient themselves from expectations of victory to what can be salvaged for the next mission. They aren't fools. This was a foreseeable outcome if the missile forts persisted, and the Chameleon shield remained strong."

Gallant said, "I agree, but we have to keep hitting the Great Ship. We can't let her catch her breath. Otherwise, she'll complete repairs and return to her former strength. Then what will we do? We'll never get another chance to finish her off."

"Our attacks have failed to inflict enough damage to compensate for our losses," said Fletcher.

He said, "The sad truth is our failure is twofold. First, the missile battery fortifications are too effective against our starfighters. And second, the strength of the Chameleon shield is too powerful for our best weapons."

She said, "We'll have to change that."

"What would you have me do?" Gallant asked.

CHAPTER 26

Fugazi

Logan said, "I've got the computer techs manufacturing one hundred microdevices. They can be installed on missiles to penetrate the Great Ship's shield. Once they're ready, we can fly them to the *Constellation*. We'll have to oversee the installation and instruct the pilots on setting the operational parameters to penetrate the shield."

Kate said, "We? Why do we have to go? Why can't the techs do it?"

"You know we're the only ones knowledgeable enough to do this job."

"I guess," she said frowning. "But how are we going to get to the task force?"

"I've commandeered an interplanetary shuttle," said Logan proudly.

"Who will fly it?"

"Me, of course. I've had basic flight training," he said haughtily.

Kate was not convinced. "What does it have for armament?"

"Nothing"

"How about stealth?"

"None."

"I'm guessing its grease lightning fast. Right?"

"No. It's a slow bucket of bolts."

Kate's jaw dropped. "How do you propose we get past the Titan raiders and reach the *Constellation*?"

"Trust me. I've got it covered," Logan bristled. "If a Titan destroyer looks interested, we play dead. We act like a dead derelict. They're too busy chasing convoys to waste time on us."

"So, your plan, to avoid admitting that I won our competition, is to get me killed?"

"Don't be childish. If you're that worried, you can remain here. I'll go alone."

Kate spent a few minutes considering that option.

"No," she said hesitantly. "I'm the one who discovered this key. It should be me who implements it. Beside some unforeseen glitches may arise, and I might be needed."

Logan breathed a sigh a relief. "Great. I'm glad you're coming."

A few hours later, Kate accompanied Logan to the spaceport.

Kate gaped. She said, "That interplanetary shuttle fits the picture of derelict perfectly."

Logan said, "Just get on board."

The inside of the vessel was as old and decrepit as the outer structure. It had a pilot and a co-pilot seat, and a single cot. Food storage and preparation were the bare minimal.

"Don't look like that," said Logan. "Think of this as one of the great mysterious adventures you're so fond of talking about."

Kate shook her head.

"Captain Gallant is sending a pair of fighters back to escort us."

"Really?" Kate brightened. "That's great."

"Yeah. They'll meet us at the edge of the asteroid field and escort us for the last leg."

"Why don't we just wait here until the escort arrives?" asked Kate.

"That would waste four days. We can't wait. The task force needs these microprocessors ASAP."

***

The first two days of Kate's journey aboard the shuttle were as uneventful as they were uncomfortable.

When they approached the edge of the asteroid field, she asked, "Where's our escort?"

Logan squirmed. "I guess they're running a little late."

"Radio them and find out when they will get here," she said in a huff.

"Can't do that. We're obeying radio silence. Using the radio would just give our position away."

"Do you see any Titan ships?"

"No. Not yet. But it's not the one you see that kills you. It's the one you don't."

Kate was unhappy, and over the next few hours, she gave Logan more dirty looks than he cared to have in a lifetime.

Finally, Logan said, "I've picked up a radar signal."

"I'm shocked that thing works. Is it our escort?" asked Kate.

"No." He frowned. "It looks like a Titan destroyer at extreme range. But I don't think he has detected us."

Logan maneuvered the shuttle closer to a large asteroid cluster. It was a complex of rocks orbiting each other which could afford them some cover.

"You watch the radar. Call out bearing and range to the destroyer," he said. "I'll try and keep the ship's radar shadow minimal. The destroyer is a lot bigger and faster than us, but in this field of rocks, we're more maneuverable."

"Contact starboard zero six. Range two light-minutes," said Kate.

"Good. Our speed is down to a crawl, but that destroyer will have a hard time getting a whiff of us."

"Contact starboard one two. Range one light-minute."

"Turning to port." Logan pulled the joystick over hard.

It was speed versus maneuverability for the two mismatched ships.

"Contact starboard zero two."

"I got this," said Logan, but the bearing was constant, while the range was closing. It was an intercept situation.

"Contact bearing starboard zero five. Range

one light-minute."

The destroyer was coming within its firing envelope.

The dance continued as each ship commander tried to outguess his opponent and fool him.

"Contact bearing port one six. Range indefinite."

"Very well," said Logan.

The two ships turned almost simultaneously. They maintained their distance as they circled the asteroid cluster. Kate felt they were getting away with Logan's tactic.

The destroyer continued to follow the very minimal radar contact it had.

"Contact bearing port one four. Range forty light-seconds."

"We're losing ground," said Kate. "Are you going to try turning again?"

"No, I don't think so."

The enemy had limitations of his own. The destroyer had a wider turning radius, but good management would lead to its success if the struggle were prolonged.

"Contact bearing port zero eight. Range one light minute."

"Very well."

The two ships were circling each other, like two children running around a tree. Sometimes running is all you can do.

The winning Titan strategy was to reverse direction before Logan realized the switch. His only defense was to reverse course simultaneously. But timing was everything. It was a matter of seconds, and any delay would be fatal. Not only was quickness of thought required, but also quickness of execution. Each decision had to be made in a split second with the reaction rate of a boxer.

The next set of radar contacts and turns seemed to show the shuttle's maneuvers were succeeding. Logan's turn was as quick as the enemy's, giving him a few seconds' advantage. He turned again, anticipating the enemy's next turn. Again, he remained safe.

"Contact bearing port zero five. Range thirty light-seconds."

That change in bearing was due to Logan's turn. The next report was vital. Logan waited tensely. He hoped the *Constellation's* fighters might be coming.

Again, they were at a constant bearing and a closing range. The rendezvous would mean only one would survive.

The Titan destroyer fired.

The missile left the destroyer's rack and soared toward the shuttle.

Logan had no jammers, no antimissiles, no countermeasures of any kind. He could only move closer to an asteroid and hope the missile became confused about its target.

Fortunately, the missile struck the nearby asteroid.

A second missile approached.

He altered course. It was a high-g brutal turn.

The odds were against him.

"Turn! Damn it! Turn!" he said.

There was nothing more to do. The missile exploded against a nearby asteroid. The shattered rock spewed fast hard stones against the shuttle's fragile frame, severely damaging it. There was a smell of acidic fumes from burning insulation. And the emergency lights took over.

Kate was frightened when she saw Logan lying unconscious on the deck.

She gathered her courage and turned off all power.

The destroyer lost interest in what was now a truly derelict vessel.

This is what alone feels like.

The shuttle was dirty and cramped, with barely enough room to crawl. She was on her knees, dragging Logan to the shelter of a bulkhead. Blood dripped from a cut over his eye.

Light seeped into the hot, smoky compartment.

She hoped Logan would wake. Tears and sweat trickled down her cheek. She bit her lip.

Finally, Logan reached out and took her hand. It was cold and clammy.

She bandaged his injuries and they rested.

After several quiet hours, Logan said, "Tell me all about the time you found the treasure chest."

Kate laughed, "Here? Now?!"

"Why not? I want to know before . . . before help arrives."

Kate blinked. "I was named Katherine at birth after my maternal grandmother. A perfectly lovely feminine name. It was a name for a delicate child who did her lessons and obeyed her elders. It was not a name for a scrawny tomboy who ran wild through the countryside, beyond our home, beyond our village. By my eighth birthday, no one referred to me by the dignified Katherine. I had become Kate. I spent my childhood exploring forests, streets, and canals. You name it. I was *curious*. It was a bright and beautiful time in my life. That's when I came across the treasure chest. When I say, 'came across,' I mean, I stole it out of my mother's bureau draw. I thought it had jewelry in it. While I was busy trying to crack the chest's lock, my mother was taken to the hospital with a stroke. She died three days later, and I never got to apologize for my theft. I kept the chest, and weeks later, I came across the key to it while packing away my mother's clothes. The chest had several love letters from my father, who had died soon after I was born. In addition, there was a single photo."

She showed him the picture she kept in her jacket pocket.

"It's all I have left of her." A tear ran down Kate's cheek. "I was like Alice falling down the rabbit hole, but I didn't feel like a child anymore. I still half-believed in fairy tales and Santa Clause, but deep down, I knew the difference between dreams and nightmares. It seems cruel, doesn't it? To have my treasure be a picture of something I desperately want and can't have."

She inched closer to Logan. "You don't think that one day, you'll look up, and your mom won't be there anymore, but if it happens, you'll find that the world's become a colder place."

The conversation died a natural death.

CHAPTER 27

Yes, We Can

Captain Gallant was elated when he learned that the escort fighters had rescued Kate and Logan. They had a cramped ride back to the *Constellation*, but they made it. And they brought a crate of microprocessors with them. His faith and trust in the pair had paid off.

Kate and Logan installed the microprocessors into the Goliath warheads and trained the pilots. Before long, the upgraded weapons were loaded onto the bombers in preparation for the next mission.

For the next few days, Gallant spent much of his time in CIC. He poured over Hawkeye scouting reports about the Great Ship's efforts to improve its defenses. He examined the details of the asteroid field to find a weakness he might exploit. But the Chameleon were resourceful and diligent in their endeavors—their repair work was going well.

Gallant gathered key officers for a briefing in CIC. The situation room inside the compartment was used for planning. The room itself measured about twenty by twenty meters. Walking in, the first thing one saw was the front wall video feeds from drones and Hawkeyes. When a screen was expanded, the monitor could display detailed images. However, there was a signal latency issue. Having access to such a sophisticated system allowed them to up their game.

Fletcher said, "CIC is the best place to examine all aspects of the battle space. We can integrate the latest intelligence reports."

Lieutenant Jacobs whined, "Why do we spend so much time planning? Isn't it better to plunge in and fight with vigor and courage? To plow ahead without suffering the anxiety of waiting. Get at the enemy and attack immediately, that's how I would do it."

"Battle is filled with enough uncertainty," said Gallant. "Giving away, what little advantage we can garner ahead of time, is foolish. Planning and training save lives and wins battles."

There was a murmur of agreement from the other officers.

The next day, Gallant devised a plan of outrageous boldness. He intended to use speed, stealth, and surprise to deliver a devastating blow. Just the sort of operation that his starfighters were eager for. He counted on Ryan and Lorelei to carry it out. Since the narrow passages through the asteroid belt caused fighters to pass close to missile batteries, he would send the Marines to clear the way.

He gathered his key officers once more.

Fletcher asked, "How are we going to solve this complex problem?"

Gallant said, "My plan is to use the Hawkeye data to pinpoint targets for the Marines."

He paused and gazed at their questioning faces. "We'll send them in on transports to assault the forts, clearing the way for a strike by the starfighters minutes later."

A few nodding heads encouraged him to continue. "Then using the microprocessors installed in the Goliath, the missiles will penetrate the Great Ship's shield and finish it off."

The officers examined the plot of the campaign he had outlined.

Gallant said, "I try to do everything right to keep people safe, but there is always that chance it's not enough. We're facing a great challenge, but no harder than we've faced before. We can't lose faith in each other."

After the briefing, the task force was ready. Hawkeyes and drones were sent to scout. The *Warrior* sped wide on the flank. Sightings, or blips, were reported and analyzed.

The *Constellation* and *Courageous* crept closer to the Great Ship's position. Steward's Marine Raider Battalion was prepared to face the dangerous mission. The battlecruiser *Indefatigable* was assigned to accompany the transports. The starfighters scrambled on the flight deck for an attack they hoped would deliver the coup' de gras.

The group of transports loaded with Marines

was on its way to attack the forts. The battlecruiser *Indefatigable* led a bombardment group in close support. The rest of Task Force 34 flanked the transport group. The carriers prepped their pilots. As impressive as these forces were, constant vigilance was imperative.

When the Marine assault force reached the forts, Task Force 34 launched its starfighters.

Time was ticking.

CHAPTER 28

Zzey

On his tenth anniversary as Commander-in-Chief of the Titan Battle Fleet, Admiral Zzey stood on the bridge of the spacecraft carrier *Vampiri* as it sailed majestically through the Ross star system. Tall and broad-shouldered, the Titan leader had alert, intelligent eyes. They revealed an individual of reserved yet aggressive temperament. True to his heritage, he was a brilliant regimented autistic savant without the emotional burden of empathy. He was a well-educated broad thinker with a pragmatic viewpoint. Logic and meticulous mathematics were his tools to solve any problem. But if he thought there was an advantage to be gained, he was unafraid to deviate from doctrine. Despite these attributes, he bore the unique character of an intellectual.

He was an admiral's admiral who believed in the principle of calculated risk, which meant inflicting greater damage on the enemy than it could on him. Reconnaissance and surprise were his most prized principles. Once he pondered his strategy at length, he would fight with total commitment.

The Titan high command had unbridled faith in him.

His flagship, the *Vampiri*, was a proud, powerful ship with a crew of great character. The carrier had been completely refurbished since its last action. To his credit, he had trained a new flock of pilots to perfection and upgraded the fleet's starfighters before undertaking this mission. His staff officers were tactically excellent. The whole fleet was in high spirits and full of confidence. But these fine carriers, impressive though they were, were merely the tip of the spear. Behind them were two monster dreadnaughts and six battlecruisers along with numerous escorts. The capital ships paraded in a formation like strutting peacocks.

Titan—Battle Fleet
Admiral Zzey
    2 Spacecraft Carriers – *Vampiri, Valkyrie*
    Starfighter Space Wing
    72 Fighters
    72 Bombers
    8 Search
  2 Dreadnought
  6 Battlecruisers
  36 Cruisers
  88 Destroyers
  88 Auxiliary Support Ships

The Titan doctrine was to expand throughout the galaxy. Anything that inhibited their access to the needed resources was an obstacle to be eliminated. Admiral Zzey's mission was to recapture the Ross system. But he faced a perplexing dilemma.

In the Gliese system, Zzey defended his home planet against both the humans and the Chameleon. Now he might be forced to defend the Chameleon from the humans. Having fought Task Force 34 before, no one knew better than him that he faced a resourceful and dangerous foe. The threat was real, but he expected to defeat them. He would have to choose his path forward with great care.

Each day, Zzey dived into his messages and workload with zeal. The messages were from fleet units and required his attention to priority issues. He was a detail person and he read every item diligently. He worked in the flagship's operational room for hours until every element was complete. His blunt forthright manner set a standard for his officers. He emphasized that they must always use clear and precise communication. After the evening meal, he returned to work until bedtime without allowing himself any time to relax. He could never depend upon uninterrupted slumber because demanding issues always arose.

Planning for the upcoming operation in the Ross system had occupied his staff for their entire journey. While he held discussions with them, his fleet moved closer to the asteroid field. The situation offered many what-ifs and alternative strategies. According to several war game simulations, there might be a misdirection plan that could fool the enemy.

Zzey conferred with his Chief-of-Staff, Captain Uuag, a large handsome Titan. He was considered very brainy, even in comparison to the best savants. He enjoyed a reputation as a forceful, vigorous attacker. Zzey considered him the absolute best of his staff officers. Uuag was fanatically loyal to Zzey and would support him in whatever plan he chose.

Together they investigated the many ship sightings and assessed the situation. Zzey wanted a decisive battle. Others might have dragged their feet, but Uuag also wanted full engagement. The planning sessions went on for many days. Since there was little communication with the Chameleon, Zzey had only tidbits of data. Their condition and intentions remained a mystery. Sorting out and interpreting communications and intensions was a puzzle. While the Chameleon knew more about the human's forces, they weren't forthcoming. Trust was at a minimum between the old enemies.

Before he could proceed, Zzey had to deal with some internal Titan politics. There was an internal staff debate about whether saving the Chameleon Great Ship was worth the loss of many fighters and ships. Perhaps the elimination of that old enemy wouldn't be missed.

Uuag said, "Sir, there is much to consider for this upcoming mission. We should start by acknowledging that there are three sides to a triangle."

"Aptly stated," grunted Zzey. "There are many layers in the strategy of war."

"The Chameleon have been our enemy for a

century. Can you consider them an ally now, just because they have switched sides?"

"Of course not. They have only flipped because the humans refused to yield the Ross system to them. We have no desire for either of these species to possess the Ross system. It's a dagger pointing into the heart of our empire."

As commander-in-chief, Zzey couldn't tolerate the thought of another attack on his home world. His ultimate fear was that Ross could become a staging point for more attacks against Gliese. He considered it his primary duty to prevent that.

"So, you will not aid the Chameleon now that they are in need?" asked Uuag.

"I said, there are layers in war. Here we must play in a three-sided game. Ask yourself, who is the greater enemy? What can we exploit to our advantage? What will be our endgame? When you have answered these questions to my satisfaction, we will have a battle plan to advance our nation in this war."

"Yes, Admiral. I will convene the fleet staff and undertake a thorough evaluation of our options for your judgment."

"Thank you, Uuag."

Zzey and his staff were not too concerned when they received news of another raid on the Great Ship. They anticipated that there would be more. The atmosphere of the fleet was good, and time was on their side.

Uuag argued with staff over the possibilities. Some thought it would be better for the Great Ship to be destroyed first, then they would deal with the depleted task force. This would eliminate their old enemy and allow them the concentrate on a new, but weaker enemy.

Or they could send their fighters to boost the Great Ship's defense, but that would leave their fleet vulnerable. The task force leader might be smart enough to take advantage of that. The Titan might pay too high a price to protect an old enemy. Fighters were the strength of the fleet and couldn't be expended without due consideration.

Or they could defend Great Ship and attack the task force together with the Great Ship when it was repaired.

Or they could try and destroy the task force regardless of the state of the Great Ship. Why not take advantage of the fact that the task force was occupied? That would make use of their old enemy to wear down their new enemy.

Each option had its advantages and disadvantages.

The staff's consensus was to let the Chameleon stew in their own juices.

A less gifted tactician than Uuag might have rested and let that be the solution, but he ran more simulations. How many starfighters might be allotted to defend the Great Ship against how many were needed to defend the fleet?

Uuag wasn't ready to commit to one strategy. Instead, he kept the options open as they move further into the star system. Zzey formally agreed with Uuag's assessment that a final decision should be postponed.

In his headquarters, Zzey began to outline some possible war plans for his commanders. Planning went into high gear. The distance and vectors of ships were calculated to precise points. He issued an unprecedented order that he would assign priority targets himself.

According to the latest information, Zzey was in a strong position—a judgment, he hoped, was correct. Timing was a straitjacket he would have to accommodate. And at some point, he would be forced to commit.

CHAPTER 29

Send in the Marines

Tick, tick, tick . . . time dragged on for Major Steward and his battalion of Marines as they prepared for the space assault. The Marines stared out the portals at the empty space around them as the transports carried them into the asteroid belt. They heard pings of small meteorites hitting the hull.

Steward had prepared his troops for this critical moment. They were ready. That didn't mean that they would do everything according to plan. There were always bumps and unexpected pitfalls. But if he planned wisely, their training would benefit them when they needed to rely on it. That's how he expected them to carry out the mission and survive. But there are certain moments when emotions can't be denied. They would have to survive those as well.

Task Force 34 remained one light-hour from the target area while the transports approached the Chameleon fortifications. As the Marines approached the jump-off point, the *Indefatigable* launched a missile bombardment.

The Marines sat in full combat gear in order of their jump rotation. They fidgeted and mumbled and grunted and told crude jokes. Sergeant McCauley stood up and walked down the aisle, inspecting the troops. He tested his communication channel and reset the signal. The rack of seats in the transport was cramped and uncomfortable, but Marines never expected comfort. Their outfits were as black as space. It offered a measure of camouflage during the drop.

The final hour passed without a sign of any uninvited guests. They were becoming restless and wanted the activity to flex their muscles. The uneasy calm continued. Sonny talked about what they were going to do on their next liberty. But the tension was always there, under the surface.

One Marine asked, "How do we take this piece of sh*t rock?"

Another asked, "Look at this place. Why are we targeting the bottom of this asteroid's crevasse? Shouldn't we be on top?"

"Do you even know which way is up in space?" laughed Sonny.

"Don't even try to make jokes, Sonny. If the Marines wanted you to laugh, they would have issued you a sense of humor. Same as everything else they gave you," said McCauley. "The temperature and vacuum of space kill more Marines than lasers or projectiles."

Meanwhile, their escort battlecruiser continued its barrage. The Marines craned their necks to get a peek out of the portals. Undoubtedly, Sonny was amused to see the fireworks going on outside. There were flashes of plasma fire in the distance.

Their faces were no happier.

Tick, tick, tick ... they were getting closer.

"Five minutes to jump point!" said McCauley.

A rustling withered through the rack of jump seats as nearly every one of the Marines shuffled in their gear.

It was time to hook up. Cobra-787 jets streamed a one-hundred-meter cable behind it. The Marines tethered to the cable as each squad of paramarines exited the transport.

The Cobras carried the Marines toward the fortification.

The Chameleon fired projectile and plasma weapons at the ships and their tails of defenseless men and women.

The first squad reached the outer fort.

McCauley screamed, "JUMP! GO! GO! GO!"

More squads launched, one after another.

The Marines pulled the release cord that freed them from the tether. They were independent now. They had to rely on their jetpack to get them the rest of the way to their targets. Each Marine had a relative position indicator to locate their target. They flew in a formation using jetpacks to keep together. They pressed the jet thruster to guide them even while they faced a hail of projectiles and plasma bolts.

Explosions and plasma flashes ripped through the group of men and women. Sometime a careening body would go wildly through the formation out of control. That Marine was lost. Sonny saw several enemy batteries firing into his group, wreaking havoc.

Several times, Sonny heard the smack of ricocheting rock fragments slam against his armor plating. He was aware that there were gaps in his battle suit armor, but he loved that armor. It kept him safe. He wanted to fire back, but the enemy was out of range of his rifle. He continued to dive toward the asteroid target, and the very steep angle of attack let him present a minimal target aspect to the batteries. He throttled back on his jetpack to avoid a wounded Marine who had lost control.

The Marines began to reach their targets, forts A, B, C, and D. Redoubt D was the greatest obstacle. Each squad of Marines fired on the enemy.

Landing on the asteroid holding fort D, McCauley yelled, "How much gear has landed?"

"Not enough, Sergeant," said Sonny.

"Heavy weapons?"

"I don't know."

"Keep behind the rocks and start firing."

A moment later, the Marines opened fire.

Pfft! Pfft! Pfft!

The Chameleon returned fire from their fortified positions. A hail of projectile bullets sprayed the Marines. The silent splat of projectiles struck the boulders, chipping off particles. Another heavy projectile weapon opened fire.

Pfft! Pfft! Pfft! Pfft! Pfft! Pfft! Pfft! Pfft! Pfft!

Sonny watched the destruction of the projectiles and hoped the battle armor he wore would protect him. But as he looked around, he saw his fellow Marines being skewered, dying one after another.

He said, "John took a hit in the face! He isn't going to make it."

McCauley said, "They're learning how to kill us. Keep moving."

Even as the sergeant spoke, Sonny's armor was pierced in a dozen places. Air escaped first. Cradling his hands to his chest, he felt like a drowning man gasping for oxygen. Then a streaming torrent of blood flew out the holes. He starred bewildered at his beloved battle armor.

"Sergeant, I need help."

McCauley stopped and scanned his personnel health monitor. He watched Sonny's vital signs decline.

"Hang on, Sonny, I'm coming."

McCauley jetted toward the wounded Marine.

"Am I going to make it?"

"Sure, kid. Sure."

"No. I can see it in your eyes."

Sonny was floating untethered in space. Darkness devoured him like a raging beast.

McCauley took a breath but in the next second, he continued the assault. He shot grappling hooks across the chasm between asteroids to ride along the wires.

Explosive charges shot the barbs across. One squad was badly shot up and fought to survive. They eventually made it back to safety.

They put out an avalanche of fire. The Marines were all over the asteroid, jumping toward the missile battery. The Marines launched a daring charge at fort D, the main defensive battery. Steward led the attack and passed through the first squad into the enemy position. The enemy resisted. A pillbox held the ground. It was the last obstacle holding the position.

The Marines broadcast messages to the Chameleon, demanding the forts' surrender. But several forts continued to fight. The situation was perfect for some die-hard units to hold out.

Though fort A did surrender, all the remaining forts chose to fight on. Redoubt D rallied, eager to demonstrate their strength.

Steward told his men this is what they'd signed up for. It was going to be much harder than they imagined, but their bulldog mentality would save them.

The Marines worked to break the defenses, but the efforts didn't last long. They couldn't stop the onslaught of projectiles. The Marines took a licking, but they were getting closer to the forts.

The Chameleon sent a barrage of missiles flying toward the battlecruiser. Their missiles were powerful and sure to cause considerable damage. Countermeasures were taken, and ships maneuvered to effect. They fired a second barrage of missiles, but now the ship turned on them and started unleashing its own power. The missiles hit the forts and dismantled them one after another. Only Redoubt D remained.

Steward radioed, "We need starfighter support to finish the job of clearing these forts."

Marines cheered when they heard that fighters were on the way.

CHAPTER 30

Battleline

When Zzey arrived at the edge of the asteroid field, he was nearing the critical point of the operation. As he reviewed the sighting reports, his confidence grew. The last attack on the Great Ship had failed. He was hopeful his arrival would forestall more attacks. But the location of the enemy task force was uncertain. He couldn't know what the enemy commander would do. Nevertheless, Zzey believed he dominated the situation.

Aboard the *Vampiri*, his crew shared his optimism and wishful thinking. He issued the premature order that the enemy was to be pursued and eliminated wherever they appeared. The significance of past Titan victories made him believe they could do anything. But the change in the quality of personnel was evident. They had lost some of their best pilots and officers in action against Task Force 34. The loss of key personnel was painful for Zzey. The training of replacements had gone well, but no amount of training can replace experience.

There was no rest for his team of analysts. They had to review the enemy movements and give recommendations. It soon became evident that his initial plan of action needed an adjustment. A less confident commander might have doubted himself. But Zzey was not reluctant to alter the operation if it meant improving his probability of success.

The Chameleon radioed, "Your immediate support is necessary for us to hold our fortified position. A new attack is starting."

The message wasn't reassuring. Zzey knew perfectly well that he couldn't count on the Chameleon to hold out indefinitely. He needed to make a difference.

Zzey was confident of ultimate victory in the Ross system. His only fear was that he might not get a chance to deliver the knockout blow to his nemesis, Task Force 34.

A search craft reported the location of enemy warships. The sighting sent the fleet to general quarters. It was reported that there were several cruisers and a half dozen destroyers leading a group of transport assault ships. A second sighting reported a large unspecified group of enemy ships one light-hour away from the Chameleon ship. This target was several light-hours away from Zzey's position.

The Titan fleet became a flurry of preparations for an attack. There was no rest until everything was attended. Course and speed were adjusted, and all ships followed in precision formation. Take-off times were set, and scouts prepared. The search ships were launched with great fanfare, and tense minutes passed, waiting for the attack group to follow. Zzey was aware that he might have to adjust plans if enemy movements were detected outside his expectations. But unless otherwise specified, the search and attack groups would complete their mission as ordered.

Zzey ordered, "Send our Phantom fighters to defend the Great Ship."

"How many do you want to send, Admiral?" asked Uuag. "I would recommend thirty-six. That will leave us a like number for our CSP."

"Make it so."

In less than an hour, Zzey added further instructions for his pilots. He wanted them to increase acceleration and close at a greater rate. In addition, he made a minor course change to the fleet. This might seem meaningless, but it represented deeper thinking about his part in the future. How significant this marginal adjustment was worth would only be determined after the action.

The cruiser *Hhavver* fell out of formation with engine trouble. It was an annoying problem that Zzey dismissed from his mind almost at once. He decided that the squadron commander would take appropriate action.

There was growing uneasy over the ambiguous sightings. Heavy interference within the thick asteroid belt caused minor course corrections.

A gnawing sense of concern struck Zzey.

Space seemed small and crowded.

CHAPTER 31

Phantoms

Lieutenant Rob Ryan couldn't believe he had to get back into Lucky 7's cockpit and face the Great Ship, yet again. Whatever troubles that had plagued him, he couldn't discount what was in front of him. His Viper was hardly functioning, his wingman was wounded, and his starfighter wing was exhausted. Could they hold together? Could he inspire them to fight once more? His failure could prove disastrous. He had to pull himself together for what was coming. It was nerve-wracking.

After the three attacks on the Great Ship, Ryan's space wing had twelve fighters destroyed and twenty-four damaged plus sixteen bombers destroyed and thirty-two damaged. There was a pile of junk parts in the shops waiting for some mechanic to miraculously revitalize them.

He could only muster twenty-four fighters and thirty-six bombers for this attack. Twelve fighters and twelve bombers were left in reserve for fleet protection. It was little enough. Nevertheless,

Ryan wished he had a few more Vipers with him.

He settled into the number two catapult.

An hour later, the wing was launched. Ryan had a few minutes to relax. Flying was a breath of fresh air compared to waiting on the flight deck. He was supporting what he hoped was the final attack. He examined the attack vector through the asteroid field.

We should have destroyed that monster by now.

But it still survived, somehow.

At the extreme port edge of the space wing, Ensign Joe Flannery reported, "Bear to Lucky; There's something suspicious several light-minutes ahead, bearing two three four."

"What is it?" asked Ryan.

"I don't know exactly. It's strange. Request permission to investigate."

"Granted."

He left formation and followed the signal. A few more minutes passed, then, "Nothing, yet. I'll warn you if I can make this out."

"Okay."

He hoped Bear understood.

Ryan pulled the throttle back and swung the ship out of formation and around to the new heading.

The others would be wondering where he was going. They just had to obey orders, and everything would be fine.

He spent the next few minutes heading toward the unknown danger. He thought about talking over the radio, but what was the point? To make him feel less alone.

Abruptly he got a computer alert. The AI was insisting on adjusting the fuel mixture to optimize the engine drive. How typical. The stupid machine couldn't know he was involved in a real dangerous situation, and the lean fuel mixture wouldn't help.

"Got anything?" asked Bear

"I'll tell you when I got something," Ryan responded angrily. But his sensors weren't resolving the blip.

Werewolf said, "The signal is confusing."

He stared out the viewport into the dark. It was impenetrable. His eyes were no better than the hi-tech detection sensors pointing out of his ship.

Ryan began strafing runs that killed many Chameleon defenders. After their assault, the forts were weakened and vulnerable. They had done considerable damage. The Marines were encouraged to close in.

Steward radioed, "We need help clearing out the remaining forts to let the bombers go on through to the Great Ship."

Ryan was shocked minutes later when his radar showed a wave of Phantoms coming in vees through the asteroids. He believed his sleek Viper made him was more than a match for any Titan pilot in their new multi-winged fighter nicknamed the Phantom. The Viper could accelerate faster and had a smaller turning radius. It was proving to be dominant, despite the Phantom's more powerful laser and plasma cannons.

Ryan yelled, "Where did they come from?!"

CHAPTER 32

Duel

Gallant's muscles were aching from sitting in an awkward position for so long. His head throbbed from the continuous mental tension, and his joints violently protested the moment he tried to move. Stiffly he repositioned himself in the command chair. How long had he been on the bridge? He missed his morning routine and his regular walkabout. He had a theory that captains who deviated from routine paid the price for the self-indulgence. It might seem important to sit for hours on the bridge—to be as near as possible should anything occur—but that meant that he was less prepared to meet a challenge should it arise.

He discretely bent and stretch, but he almost groaned as the sore muscles strained. He plopped back in his chair. He was immediately struck with a desire for cups and cups of hot coffee. But the target reports were changing and closing. He forced his weary brain to concentrate and try to guess the enemy's next move.

The United Planets was the underdog against two alien races, the Chameleon and Titans, bent on the elimination of humans. They had size, power, and interstellar footprint to make their desires real. The battle over the Ross system was a pivotal moment in the war between them.

Henry Gallant had done his share to keep his people in the game. Less than two years after he defeated the Titans in Ross and then in Gliese, they were back for a rematch. This time the aliens were working together. This was the next salvo in the war intended to bring all conflict to a conclusion. But events were not conforming to the aliens ideal. The Great Ship had been wounded and needed repair and protection.

The complicated Ross battle situation was actually several battles at once. The Marines were fighting in the asteroid belt while the starfighters attacked the Great Ship. And Task Force 34 stood guard against Titan intervention. Each battle would have its own resolution, and only the successful conclusion of all three would be decisive.

Gallant waited while the *Constellation* steadied herself on the new heading. Task Force 34 was poised to strike against any interloper.

After the terrible damage from its meeting with the Great Ship, it was miraculous that the *Constellation* was ready for action. The spirit throughout the task force was strong. Mere material strength doesn't always win—the fiber of those in the battle matter as well. A ship of war is a machine no more powerful than the crew. There were intangible assets.

There was not the least doubt that they would be victorious.

Gallant's knowledge of the enemy position and intensions was still vague, but he intended to meet them whatever the case. He wouldn't underestimate them.

There had been a series of false sightings throughout the watch. Now they needed to get a serious evaluation. He sent Hawkeyes to sweep space with extra care, but space is big.

The *Constellation* had been monitoring enemy activity all day long. The Marines had landed on the asteroids and were engaged with the Chameleon forts and missile batteries. Ryan reported that starfighters were halfway to their target, the Great Ship. And now there were reports of Titan ships approaching the region. The strain of keeping track of all these events was wearing on Gallant. Yet he had to keep his mind active and engaged. He had to find solutions to an endless litany of problems as fast as they appeared. He had no idea how the crew was bearing up. Once again, the break in his routine was costing him physically and mentally.

"I've been relieved, sir," said Lieutenant Neilson, interrupting Gallant's train of thought. The midwatch was over. The task force had made progress, but the hours had passed, partly in misery, and partly in worry waiting for the latest battle reports.

"Lieutenant Carlson is now Officer of the Deck."

That's good. He's a good man.

"Very well, Mr. Neilson," said Gallant. He looked at the young man and recognized the same stiff muscles and tense expression that he wore. "Get some rest while you can."

"Aye aye, sir."

Gallant watched the officer disappear through the hatch.

Rest? That would be nice.

"Mr. Carlson!"

"Yes, sir?"

"Extend the search perimeter, another light-minute. Let's get some resolution on these targets sitting at extreme range."

"Aye aye, sir."

A few minutes later, Carlson reported, "Hawkeye-7 reports confused sensor indications, sir."

Disappointed, Gallant said, "Keep me informed."

"Aye aye, sir."

He didn't want to impose an extra burden on the men and women of his crew, but there was little opportunity to give them a rest. He was fortunate to have such an excellent crew aboard the *Constellation*, but they had a breaking point. It was up to him not to exceed it.

Considering breaking points, he had one too. He decided that he needed a shower and a fresh uniform if he was going to appear respectable. It was time for a breather.

"I'm going below for a few minutes. Call me immediately if there is news."

"Aye aye, sir," said Carlson.

Gallant got up and lurched off the bridge. His cramped legs barely carried him to his cabin. His bloodshot eyes blinked against the cabin lights. He wanted to throw himself facedown onto the cot. He needed sleep, but that would be impossible. The thought crossed his mind that maybe he could rest his eyes for an hour. That, too, was impossible.

He stripped off his clothes and stepped into the shower. He let the hot water ricochet off his aching muscles. It felt good. He felt guilt enjoying it when there were so many pressing things to deal with. He only allowed himself five minutes before he dressed. The brief interval away from the bridge offered him a moment to think about things other than aliens.

An image of Alaina flashed in his mind.

"Captain to the bridge!" bleared the intercom. "Captain to the bridge!"

What?

He had only been away a few minutes.

Sprinting to the bridge, he heard, "Captain, Hawkeye-7 reports an uncertain contact. The range is indefinite, bearing approximately two three five," said Carlson.

"Is that the only new contact since I went below, Mr. Carlson?"

"Yes, sir."

"Any word from the starfighters?"

"They aren't scheduled to strike for another ten minutes, sir. They were ordered to maintain radio silence until then."

"Quite right. Quite right." Gallant rubbed his crusty eyes.

"You look like you could use this, sir," said the XO. She handed him a mug of coffee.

Gallant took the mug of hot coffee, its aroma quaffing up into the air. He swallowed two great gulps before setting the mug down. "Thanks, XO. You're right as always."

She grinned. "The Marines have engaged the forts and are making some progress, but they're facing problems. The starfighters should engage in ten minutes. However, I'm concerned about this latest Hawkeye report of a faint contact reading at long distance. It's probably Titan raiders, but you never know."

Gallant looked puzzled then he remembered. He pulled up the chart on his monitor. He said, "This target could be a continuation of the old contact. The reports follow its course from the outer system directly toward the Great Ship's location."

"Exactly, sir. All the old faint contact reports trace a course to reinforcement to the Great Ship. It could be one of the Titan cruiser-destroy raider squadrons. Or..."

Their discussion was interrupted by a report from CIC.

"Phantoms are attacking the Marines and our starfighters."

Gallant and Fletcher stared at each other for a second.

"Where did they come from?" asked the XO.

"I was wondering if the Titan might up their game. There must be a Titan Battle Fleet in the Ross system," said Gallant.

The XO said, "We don't have a definite identification of the enemy ships. Only speculative targets at this point."

"Our first order of business is to acquire an accurate picture of the enemy."

The XO said, "I'll send additional Hawkeyes out."

Gallant said, "Is there anything we've overlooked? Anything more we can do?"

"We've prepared everything we can think of."

Twenty minutes later, Hawkeye-7 reported, "Large number of enemy ships bearing two three six range one light-hour."

The XO demanded, "What ships? Where are the carriers?"

Gallant said, "If that is the carrier force, we need to be prepared."

Ten minutes later, Hawkeye-7 reported, "Many enemy ships."

The XO said, "Didn't they specify how many or give their course and speed?"

"No, Ma'am," said the OOD.

"Haven't we trained the search pilots on how to do their jobs?" asked the XO in frustration.

"Maybe their equipment isn't performing or perhaps they're too excited," said Gallant in a soothing tone.

Hawkeye-8 reported, "Large flight of enemy

fighter heading toward the Great Ship in the asteroids."

Gallant had heard enough. It was time to act.

"OOD go to general quarters."

"Aye aye, sir."

"General quarter! General quarters! Man your battle stations."

Gallant ordered, "Send additional CSP out."

A new fear wormed its way into Gallant's psyche in a malicious, treacherous fashion. Something spooky was going on. It might be the worst possibility he could imagine—a Titan battle fleet arriving to save the Great Ship and destroy Task Force 34.

His mind quickly inventoried the remaining starfighters aboard the *Constellation* and the *Courageous*. Where had he deployed the battlecruiser? How many ships could the Titans afford to commit to the Ross system? Would they send Admiral Zzey against him once more?

Although any alien reinforcements might arrive too late. If Ryan could get the job done. It was too late to make new arrangements.

Wasn't it?

The Titans' admiral would have his own worries. Zzey would send his own starfighters to support the Great Ship, but that would leave him few starfighters to send against Task Force 34. Timing. It was all a matter of timing. Gallant conjured up a picture of the asteroid field with the Great Ship, the center target.

Somehow, I must . . .

His meanderings were interrupted.

The OOD said, "Hawkeye-7 reports many Titan ships distance one light-hour, bearing two three six, mark 2. Ships include at least one carrier."

Gallant was on his feet again. It was his greatest fear—realized.

Carlson said, "More target sightings coming in fast from drones and other Hawkeyes, sir. It's a Titan battle fleet consisting of two carriers and several dreadnaughts. And a gaggle of starfighters is heading toward the Great Ship."

Gallant took a deep breath. If he abandoned the attack on the Great Ship, he could divert those starfighters against the Titan fleet. After all, the Titan fleet was now the more immediate threat. But switching orders while Ryan's ships were already engaged would cause confusion. He didn't know what kind of shape Ryan's forces were in. He could wreak havoc with them, and they would not only fail to finish the Great Ship, but they would be easy prey for the Titans.

Fighting frustration and baffling options, he resisted the urge to act simply because he felt the need to do something. The tension almost made him lose patience. He imposed his self-control, forcing away the blurry confusion and focusing on those things that he could do. This was a pivotal moment. He had to take the time to think clearly. Whatever he did, it had to be right.

Which way would Zzey turn? Toward the asteroids or toward the task force? He had to take the options away from Zzey. He had to force him to turn toward the task force. There were innumerable things to do. In some ways, this battle was the reverse of the one Gallant had fought before.

"Helm, come to course 060, mark 2."

"Come port to course 060, mark 2, aye, sir."

"Sir, on course 060, mark 2."

"Very well."

"Contact, 090, one light-hour, sir. Designate contact, Tango 21, sir."

"Very well."

The fiery XO urged an immediate retaliation.

On *Constellation*, Gallant and his staff studied the implications of confronting the Titan Fleet. His starfighters were depleted and exhausted. He reviewed the sighting reports of the Titan fleet moving in the star system. He anticipated the arrival of Titan fighters to support the Great Ship.

How could he interdict that?

He suspected that he once more faced Admiral Zzey, an exceptionally talented commander. Their starfighters would, no doubt, tangle long before a ship-to-ship action occurred.

He concluded that Zzey had sent several of his squadrons to help the Great Ship. They were minutes too late. They did, however, shoot up some starfighters that engaged the stubborn resisting forts.

Gallant hesitated. He had faced Zzey before. He was resilient and resourceful.

At least this time, he wouldn't have any trouble locating his enemy. He knew exactly where

the Titan fleet was, and they knew where he was.
    It was just a matter of timing.
    His and Zzey's.

CHAPTER 33

Death to the Beast

Kate balled her fists and clenched her jaw. She spat, "Damn Logan! This is all his fault."

"What was that?" asked Kelsey.

"Nothing. Never mind," said Kate, her eyes blazing. "I was reminding myself how I came to be sitting in Hawkeye-1, ten-light minutes from the Great Ship."

"Well, I, for one, am overjoyed that you're here. You have a vital role to play."

"I'm a scientist. I work in a laboratory. I'm not into space battles, you know."

"Tuning the Goliath warheads to the optimal frequency may make all the difference."

"I already programmed the frequencies into the microprocessors. I don't think my being here is necessary."

"Logan said that your work was based on simulation studies—that there was room for error—and that a last-minute adjustment might be needed."

"Yeah. He would say that," said Kate, looking

thoroughly disgusted.

"That's not true?"

"It's possible. I guess. But I just don't think I'm the one to do it. Logan, or one of the techs, should be here instead."

"Really? Captain Gallant said that only you could do this. It was too important to entrust to anyone else."

"He said that?" asked Kate wide-eyed.

"Yes, he did. And I believe him"

Somewhat placated, Kate sighed. "Okay. Let me analyze the shield signal you're detecting."

Kate spent the next few hours working with the Hawkeye AI computer chewing through the real-time signal data. Finally, she said, "Here is the optimal frequency. You need to radio the *Constellation* and have the Goliaths' input setting adjusted as they are loaded onto the Vipers."

"Great. I'll send the message."

Kate asked, "Are we going back to the *Constellation* now?"

"Oh, no. We'll wait here for the next few hours until the space wing comes for its attack."

"Then what?"

"Kate, you're in Hawkeye-1. We will be updating the attack trajectory and directing the electronic countermeasures throughout the battle."

"Will we get *very* . . . close? Do you think? To the actual fighting, I mean?"

"Kate, we'll be in the eye of the storm."

***

At 0830, Lorelei Steward reached the bombers' staging point, three-light-minutes from the asteroid fortifications. Far off to one side, a subtle change in the asteroids' motion caused her to order her squadrons to adjust course. The path through the asteroid field was hazardous. It was a daunting computer problem that required constant updates from Hawkeye-1.

One of the bombers reported a hot-running engine. Lorelei ordered it to slow down and fall out of formation. She instructed the squadron to reduce speed to conserve engine temperature and lean the mixture of anti-matter. This improved the struggling power plant's efficiency.

She received fresh targeting information from Hawkeye-1. It included data about mines and batteries. She familiarized herself with the targeting holograph of the Great Ship. The vital target areas were identified, as well as the civilian population centers to avoid. She felt better with the updated microprocessors installed on the Goliath warheads. She hoped they would reward her efforts with solid hits.

The bombers followed the course for five minutes. She was following a safe route through the rocks. She hoped the Marines had success silencing the forts.

At 0840, Hawkeye-1 transmitted updated information about the minefield. Ryan's fighters blasted a lane through the hazard. Then the fighters turned their efforts to support the Marines in their assault against the forts.

At 0850, Lorelei directed the bomber squadrons through. After a quick look at her plotting monitor, she decided to swing the bomber squadron a few degrees to port. This skirted the outer missile batteries, an adjustment that could prove fateful. Every decision was pregnant with consequence.

Lorelei radioed Kelsey in Hawkeye-1, "Nightbird, this is Flame; I need a datalink for ECM delivery over the target."

Kelsey said, "Wait."

A moment later, Kelsey made an emergency broadcast to all starfighters, "Bogies! Many Bogies approaching from sunward."

"Bogies? Where?" asked Ryan.

"Bogies? What ships are those?" asked Lorelei.

All the starfighters were alive with chatter.

A few seconds later, Kelsey reported, "The bogies are Phantoms on an intercept course with our forces."

"Nightbird, this is Flame, how did they get here?"

"I don't have that information. There must be a Titan carrier supporting the Great Ship. I recommend that fighters intercept the enemy. Course 230, mark 2."

"Nightbird, this is Lucky; roger that," said Ryan. "All fighters form up on me."

Ryan messaged Major Steward, "Sorry, to leave

the party, I have business elsewhere."

Steward replied, "We're going to miss you. Hurry back."

Ryan's Vipers threw themselves in front of the Titans. While the fighters engaged in a heated dogfight, the bombers proceeded to strike the Great Ship. Ryan's starfighters attacked the asteroid fortification while Lorelei's bombers launched the upgraded Goliath missiles at the Great Ship.

"We have a real target. Let's strike it now."

The starfighters vectored toward the enemy position.

Bear said, "I'm picking up the enemy fighters."

Werewolf said, "Skipper, I have multiple targets, bearing zero one zero, range three light-minutes."

"Squadrons 6 and 8 disengage from the enemy forts. Prepare to face enemy fighters. Regroup into formation Alpha-3," ordered Ryan.

It took several minutes to regroup but then Ryan said, "We're going in. Stay in tight. Attack."

He saw five fighters swing in behind him. He noticed the enemy division of ships speed ahead at a steep angle. He zoomed past them and climbed away when he didn't have the support of his wingman. Where was he?

He continued diving full throttle toward the fort. But a damaged controller sent him spiraling to port. Working frantically, he managed to pull out of it, and leveled off out of range of the battery. Then he headed back to the *Constellation*. He was useless now. He radioed permission to land, and the station gave him a Roger.

He hoped the ship had an easy fix and he could return to the battle.

The next fighter followed his approach with similar results. He limped home as well.

The Great Ship joined the forts in opening fire. They put a wall of fire in front of Lorelei's bombers. Explosions and plasma filled the space in a symphony of destruction.

One bomber was hit by a missile and fell out of formation. Lorelei ordered it to return to the *Constellation* despite protests from the pilot.

The largest defensive fort was three light-seconds from the Great Ship. It threw up a withering barrage of missiles and plasma fire.

Lorelei ordered a responding salvo of Mongoose anti-missiles. She gripped her joystick and let her mind concentrate on the neural net receptors to get a mental picture of the battlespace.

Several more bombers died in flames. More missiles found their targets, and bombers exploded.

The motion of the asteroid field obscured the bow of the Great Ship. As the bomber Squadrons 8 and 9 approached from their vantage point; there was no doubt that the Great Ship's point defenses were focused on them.

The Beast again used her guns against the bombers forcing them to disperse temporarily but could not break up the attack. There was a last-minute attempt for the ship to shift its point-defense fire to the bombers, but it was too late.

No one would have called Lorelei hesitant, least of all herself. She was aggressive and willing to take a risk when the time was right. Her fierce competitiveness was indicative of this behavior. Never-the-less, she couldn't be called reckless. An adjective she had often attributed to Ryan. Here was a situation where she might reverse those roles. Although the enemy fire was more effective than usual, Lorelei pressed her luck and led her bombers straight into it.

She ordered, "All flights follow me in echelon formation."

She swung in a wide turning motion. The elaborate swing opened the door for her squadron to reach the enemy's most vulnerable spot.

It was as decisive a situation as she had ever been involved in. She wanted to get her pilots back from this mission, yet it was important to push the limits of risk in this situation.

Lorelei ordered, "Launch Goliaths!"

Squadron 8 broke into three flights, each focused on the target specification laid out in the mission briefing. Squadron 8 launched immediately.

At 0902, Goliath missiles were on track to

the Great Ship. They maneuvered through the Great ship's countermeasures.

The Bletchley Circle technology worked perfectly. Squadron 8's Goliaths penetrated the Beast's shield. The Goliaths scored many direct hits. One warhead penetrated the ship's deck between turrets but failed to explode. A second hit amidships causing severe damage. A large hole was blown in the ship's side. An entire section of the armor belt buckled. A third warhead struck the engine room. Several more warheads blew the super-laser apart.

Quickly, the explosions penetrated the hull and set the inner compartments of the ship ablaze. The missiles that followed found soft targets and wreaked havoc inside the Great Ship.

At 0912, the Squadron 9 followed and found the going just as successful. Thirty-two bombers attacked the ship with Goliaths. Its targeting package found a soft spot. But they were slightly off-angle and exposed. After the previous attacks, where missiles explode harmlessly on the shield, this was a triumph. It seemed that every missile hit its mark, twisting the steel hull into artistic sculpture.

Hit after hit made a neat expanding hole in the hull and penetrated deeper into the infrastructure with every blast. The hits were fatal. A cascade of domino explosions indicated that internal explosions within the ship were now occurring. The Great Ship's fuel and ammunition dumps were exploding, tearing the ship in a furious self-mutilating process. Flaming debris killed everyone on the ship's bridge and control room. The Goliath bombs had penetrated the ship's heavy armor, exited the keel, and exploded in the bottom. The concussive shock caused severe damage to fire-control equipment.

In some ways, it was the complete reversal of the previous action. Forts and missile batteries were completely ineffective. It was so complicated that it was really several battles rolled into one. The last mission proved an unpalatable heavy dose of humility. It hadn't rocked their faith in the ultimate mission.

The missiles' impacts had not been felt through the ship, but the internal explosions shook the structure to its foundation. The amidship hits caused more damage. Escape pods and shuttle of people fled from the ship. There were brave Chameleons everywhere trying to put out fires and restore air pressure. But they were as a finger in the dyke.

In ten minutes, Captain Falcon issued the order to abandon ship. This appeared to stabilize the panic temporarily. Eight minutes later, a large explosion rocked the engine room. The structure was thrown. The Beast rapidly lost control functions.

The defensive fire from the point defenses vanished. It had to resort to life-saving measures instead. The mass movement of the internal population was underway. People were being moved from depressurized compartments to inner regions of stability. The crew stopped fighting and devoted all efforts to escape and rescue. The departing starfighters surveyed the destruction they had visited upon the Great Ship. Broken titanium frames and ruptured compartments bleeding air were obvious. A gaping hole in the ship's side a dozen kilometers long stood out. Despite the ship's devastation, escape pods and escape shuttles belched forth. The loss of life was heavy, but already rescue teams were helping. The living quarters had been spared from the direct attacks, and a large portion of the inhabitants remained safe awaiting rescue.

The bombers had accomplished in thirty minutes what had eluded them for thirty days. But they did not escape without a great many losses.

The Great Ship was now an abandoned derelict, flailing like an overturned turtle.

The Chameleon broadcast in the clear, "We surrender! We ask for quarter. We surrender!"

"We got 'em," screamed Lorelei. "The Beast is dead."

The fighters remained engaged with the Phantoms long enough for the bombers to do their job. Then it was time to go back to the barn. The bombers head for the *Constellation*, while the fighters covered their retreat.

Ryan didn't see the Phantom that fired a missile a mere one light-second behind his Viper. But through his neural interface, the AI shrieked, . . .

INCOMING! TAKE EVASIVE ACTION!
INCOMING! TAKE EVASIVE ACTION!

"Damn it!" he yelled.

He pushed the thrust lever forward and jerked the joystick hard over.

Using every bit of expertise, he wrestled the Viper away from the acquisition track of the missile. His vision narrowed as he pulled more g's than any other time in his life.

The missile continued to zoom toward him.

INCOMING! LAUNCH ECM!

INCOMING! LAUNCH ECM!

He smacked the decoy release button.

He whacked the electronic jamming gear switch.

In a blink of an eye, he was out of options—and time.

BRACE FOR IMPACT!

EJECT! EJECT!

It happened that fast.

Lieutenant Rob Ryan's luck had run out.

CHAPTER 34

The Curtain Falls

"Captain on the bridge," said Lieutenant Carlson.

Gallant said, "As you were."

The bridge crew continued their busy activities.

Flopping into his command chair, Gallant asked, "Do you have the returning starfighter roster?"

"Right here, sir," said Fletcher, seemingly appearing out of nowhere. "Our people did a fantastic job. The Beast is dead. The entire crew is relieved. We should plan for a celebration."

Gallant pushed back into his cushion. His doleful eyes belied his casual posture. "I agree that it's great news, but let's leave the celebrating until later. For now, give me the bad news."

"It's not good, sir." She handed him a tablet with a frightfully long list of casualties.

Lieutenant Rob Ryan's name was at the top.

"Ryan?"

"His fighter took a direct hit." Fletcher said

quietly into Gallant's ear, "No escape pod was reported."

Gallant felt a sharp pain in his chest. It extended down his left arm. He took a deep breath, trying to gather his thoughts. He hadn't experienced such a visceral reaction to the loss of a shipmate since Midshipman Michael Gabriel's death. He considered Ryan as almost a younger brother—someone to be nurtured and cared for. The responsibility for his death weighed heavily.

Fletcher waited a minute and then continued with her battle assessment. She said, "Many starfighters were lost. Those remaining are in desperate need of repair. We have no way to make up for losses in ships and crew. I'm dismayed that...,"

She broke off when she realized Gallant wasn't paying attention.

"Should I come back later?" she asked.

"No. No," said Gallant shaking his head. "We have work to do. Carry on."

Gallant examined the task force position on the display. The carriers and four destroyers were in line-ahead traveling at ten percent light speed. On their sunward side was the battleline. His battleline consisted of the *Indefatigable* and *Inflexible* with six cruisers and twenty destroyers in line-ahead. Far afield were *Warrior* to port and *Invidia* to starboard.

Task Force 34 wasn't much when he compared it to the Titan fleet. He estimated that Admiral Zzey's two carriers were supported by a battleline of at least two dreadnaughts and six battlecruisers with many more cruisers and destroyers than he cared to consider.

He reviewed the list of starfighters on the *Constellation* and *Courageous*. There were a total of 22 fighters, 26 bombers, and 5 Hawkeyes combat-ready —much less than the 72 fighters and 72 bombers at Zzey's disposal.

He narrowed his brow to concentrated on constructing a plan.

What leverage do I have? he wondered.

He had to find some. He couldn't afford to match battlelines at one light-minute. The sheer weight of numbers and throw weight would prevail. It would be a disaster. And likewise, he couldn't afford a long-distance slugging match between starfighters. His ships and crews were exhausted, and despite the success of defeating the Great Ship, morale was not good.

"I don't believe anyone has ever seen the likes of a battle such as this," said Fletcher.

"Don't worry," said Gallant. "Space battles are violent but brief. Ships travel at 0.3 lightspeed while hurtling antimatter warheads at one another. Eventually, they either obliterate each other or speed away."

"What chance do we have?" asked Fletcher.

"We have as much chance of mauling the enemy as they have against us. Don't worry. I know almost exactly what I have to do."

Fletcher flinched.

A moment later, a reconnaissance report

came in from CIC.

"There they are!" reported the Hawkeye-12. "It's the Titan battle fleet."

Gallant examined the transmitted plot for a moment and frowned. He leaned closer to examine the red dots on the display, but the comsat vectors were indistinguishable.

"Two recon drones are picking up the enemy fleet, as well," reported Jacobs from CIC.

The enemy battleline was forty light-minutes away and moving closer. It was nearer than Gallant thought.

Fletcher shook her head. "We can never hope to stop so much firepower."

Gallant said, "Carlson, send the ships to general quarters."

"Aye aye, sir."

CLANG! CLANG! CLANG!

The crew rushed to their stations, tensed for what was coming.

Gallant said, "Carlson, order the *Warrior* to scout the enemy battleline. The Titans won't see that stealthy killer in their blind spot."

He sat straight up against the back of his chair and looked at Fletcher.

Gallant said, "XO, patch together every starfighter you can. We're sending everything we have at them."

"Who will lead the attack?" asked Fletcher.

"I will," said Gallant. "I'll take twelve fighters and twenty-six bombers to attack the Titan fleet. I'm afraid you'll have to stay here and face whatever Admiral Zzey throws at you."

He paused for a moment before adding, "I can only leave you ten fighters for CSP. You might be able to patch a few more together, but that's it."

Fletcher's shocked expression slowly waned into acceptance. "It'll have to do," she said. "You can count on us, Captain."

Then she extended her hand and whispered, "Good luck, Henry."

CHAPTER 35

Everything Ends

With supreme confidence, Admiral Zzey led the Titan battleline steadily forward, closing the range to the humans. He was certain that he faced an exhausted enemy with depleted fighter strength. They wouldn't be able to put up a serious fight. He would be as a wave pounding the shore.

Chief-of-Staff, Captain Uuag, stood beside him on the bridge of the *Vampiri*. He prodded, "Admiral, our surveillance drones show the enemy at forty light-minutes. We are well within our starfighter's attack radius."

Zzey sighed but said nothing.

"Sir, we've identified the enemy task force. It is one we've faced before. We should not underestimate this enemy's leadership or strength."

"Yes, I know this commander," said Zzey, knitting his brow. "He is intelligent and logical."

"Yes, sir. But he has also proven to be quite cunning. We can not be certain he will follow an orthodox strategy."

"Humph," muttered Zzey. He despised the human's tactics, but he recognized that they had proven painfully correct more than once.

Uuag moved closer and whispered, "The consequence of overestimating such an enemy seems less..." he paused, "than underestimating him."

"Why are you so hesitant? Are you frightened of this human?"

Uuag recoiled. "No, sir. I am merely expressing an appreciation of human ingenuity."

"Human ingenuity? I never heard you speak like this before."

"This commander is different."

"Nonsense. He has been tricky. I'll grant you that. But fortune has been kind to him. Don't overestimate his abilities. He is, after all, only human."

"Of course, Admiral. Please forgive me."

Zzey moved close to Uuag. Towering over him, Zzey starred into his eyes.

Uuag immediately lowered his head and cast his eyes to the deck.

"Don't worry, Captain," said Zzey. "Our opponent is overmatched. We have more and fresher starfighters, and our battleline has a throw weight advantage of ten-fold."

Several minutes passed in silence. Then Uuag said, "Sir, we haven't been able to re-establish communication with the Great Ship. We don't know if the last attack was ineffective or not. Perhaps, the Great Ship will soon recover and join us in battle. If that were possible, it might be better for us to withdraw and await events."

"What! Withdraw and leave the battlespace to the humans? Outrageous," growled Zzey. "Our phantoms will return soon. Then we will have a complete report on the status of the Chameleon."

"Our Phantom's commander has reported many losses," said Uuag meekly.

"I assume they gave a good account of themselves," retorted Zzey, "and that the humans suffered more. That is good. It is as I said. The human fleet is a spent force."

Uuag said, "Sir, our Phantoms are still an hour away. If you are determined to engage the enemy carriers, we have time to launch a full strike of twenty-four fighters and sixty-four bombers immediately."

Zzey remained quiet for a minute. "That would leave only twelve fighters for CSP until we recover the returning Phantoms."

"You said yourself, sir, the enemy is a spent force," said Uuag. He licked his lips and added, "He will be unable to mount a significant attack on our fleet. Besides, we will be recovering the returning Phantoms soon. Once they are serviced and rearmed, they will add to our CSP. That will be enough to deal with anything we could face."

"That is a good argument," said Zzey, gazing at his chief of staff with a fresh appreciation.

Uuag held his head high and threw back his shoulders.

"What I want most is for our battleline to engage the enemy," said Zzey. He rubbed his hands together and added, "That would be a glorious sight."

The entire bridge crew turned their attention to their commander-in-chief with smiles as broad as his own.

Zzey basked in the adulation.

He was annoyed once more when Uuag said, "Sir, if we launched a strike now and crippled the enemy's task force, it would be but a trifle to bring the remnants under our guns."

"I don't know," said Zzey, wagging his head from side to side. He smacked his fist into his palm. "I want this battle to be decisive."

Uuag said, "Sir, may I suggest...,"

Zzey cut in, "Why not bring the Phantoms aboard first while we continue to close the distance to the enemy?"

"That will give the enemy time...," started Uuag.

"But we will be able to unleash our full power all at once from short range," countered Zzey. "Our starfighters will strike the enemy while the battleline is close enough to finish them off. That way, they won't have a chance to flee."

Uuag bowed his head and frowned. Surrendering the will to resist, he said, "A perfect plan, Admiral."

An hour later, the Phantoms began landing aboard the *Vampiri* and the *Valkyrie*. The strike-ready force of twelve fighters and sixty-four bombers was pushed to the side. The flight decks of both carriers were cluttered with returning fighters being moved to service ports and rearming stations. The overcrowding of starfighters became a logistical nightmare as they were stacked in every corner. Numerous warheads were scattered about as rearming continued. The crews worked feverishly to reorganize the hangers and decks to restore order.

The combat space patrol of twelve fighters broke into three flights circling the fleet.

The enemy task force was twenty light-minutes away.

Sensor operator, "Contact bearing 330, undetermined range."

Zzey said, "All ships turn away from the incoming enemy."

The Titan fleet turned.

Zzey said, "Clear the flight decks. Launch standby fighters. Bring all combat-ready fighters to the catapults."

Titan scout reported, "Enemy fighters. Bearing zero two eight. Range three light-minutes."

"Is that all the information?"

The sensor operator reported, "Incoming starfighters are twelve fighters and twenty-four bombers."

The OOD reported, "The enemy is approaching our battlefleet."

He added, "This is the strangest formation of starfighters I have ever witnessed."

"What do you mean?" asked Zzey.

The sensor operator said, "The bombers and

fighters are nested together into several integrated units. They are in the tightest grouping imaginable. I don't understand how the individual pilots can maneuver while packed together without colliding. The formation moves like one organism rather than forty ships."

The OOD said, "It's as if one mind was flying the formation instead of forty separate beings."

"Fascinating," said Zzey.

With complete emotional detachment, Zzey asked, "Could this remarkable ability make a difference?"

Uuag opened his mouth but failed to reply. Instead, he cast his gaze at the Titan lead dreadnaught, looking unstoppable with its bright armor.

Zzey asked, "How are they doing this?"

Uuag said, "They must be using a command data-link network to coordinate the space wing. It would take unbelievable AI talent to direct the mission. The forty starfighters are melded together by a linked neural net acting as a single unit. There must be a single mind controlling the entire starfighter wing. The bombers are acting like fists to pound us while the fighters shield them."

"We've never had an indication that they possessed this type of ability," said Zzey. "I hadn't considered this."

The OOD said, "Enemy starfighters are splitting into two separate groups. They can't be from one carrier. There must be more."

"One flight is going straight for the *Valkyrie*,"

reported the sensor operator.

The Titan CSP fighters engaged the enemy fighters, which tried to cover their bombers.

OOD said, "Admiral, enemy starfighters approaching *Valkyrie*."

The CSP missiles burst out. But the human bombers dove and launched multiwarhead antimatter Goliath weapons.

"Incoming enemy missiles!" called the carrier.

They ripped through and punched holes in the *Valkyrian*. A deadly chain reaction engulfed the ship. The Mangled hull was left streaming air and burping steel. Damage control teams labored against overwhelming destruction fighting a mounting tide of failed gear. The crew was no longer able to fight. The tragedy became one-sided.

The Titans appeared paralyzed by the setback. They were reassessing their strength.

"How many are there?" asked one CSP pilot.

"Too many," said another.

"It's going to be a tough ride."

The fighters reformed to cover the gaps left by the ships falling out of formation due to damage or destruction. They had been battered useless.

"It's a tough mission profile," said one pilot.

In the confused chatter of the dogfight, it was hard for Zzey to distinguish the calls for help.

"A clear kill! It lit up and was gone. We might stop them, after all."

The human starfighters blew passed the first Titan fighter defense.

The chatter over the radio was confused and overlapping. The starfighters deployed and swooped in for a strike.

An officer reported, "Our CSP has failed against their first attack."

Another officer reported, "The *Valkyrie* has been hit. It is battling to survive."

"The enemy is a Juggernaut."

The OOD reported, "The second enemy group is coming this way."

Zzey rallied his forces. The CPS moved as fast as possible to close the distance. On the bridge, he gave instructions to his pilots. He launched his fighters. He sent all available.

Uuag said, "We are launching fighters as fast as possible."

Zzey said, "Your advice has wasted my time."

A scout reported, "Two carriers and support at bearing 300, range eighteen light-minutes."

"Ready our strike force," ordered Zzey.

He knew the United Planets wasn't ready to receive an attack. And this would be his best chance to reverse fortunes. But he knew a sortie had little chance of launching. The decision was made on unsound tactical reasoning.

Uuag said, "We can't do that right now. There is chaos on the flight decks."

The carrier shuddered under the bombers' assault. The odds were changing. The human's destructive warheads guaranteed kills. But the projections indicated some enemy capital ships might survive if they fled now.

Another dreadnaught was hit.

Targeting priorities changed for the fast and agile fighters.

OOD reported, "Sir, the *Valkyrie* has been hit and left a burning wreck." Spherical projections emanated from its tortured twisted steel body, leaving an untenable hulk.

Despite Zzey's crews' valor and skill, the situation continued to deteriorate. The cruisers floated above the dreadnaughts, screening them from missiles. They were ready for another advance. Casualty reports were grim. They got a hit.

"Look at that ship explode," reported one officer, as the humans battered ship after ship into wreckage.

Zzey ran out of options.

He asked himself, "What went wrong?"

Perhaps, another commander could have stopped this.

Zzey turned to Uuag and said, "I may have miscalculated."

Another bombing attack approached the *Vampiri*. A series of Goliath warhead struck the carrier's flight deck. A chain-reaction followed as the warheads in the rearming stations detonated as well. The *Vampiri* burst into a tremendous ruby glowing ball of flame. It was a spectacular sight.

The Titan carriers were gone along with many of their escorts.

As he died, Zzey recognized the stunning defeat as a nightmare of smashed ships and struggling men lost in fiery space.

The command of the Titan battleline was transferred to the commander of the lead dreadnaught. With both the Titan carriers destroyed and many of his capital ships damaged. He knew it was necessary to retreat from the Ross star system.

CHAPTER 36

Buttons and Bows

A month after the rout of the Titans, a shuttlecraft left the *Constellation*, heading toward Charlie. An hour later, Gallant stepped out of a ground car in front of the governor's mansion. A dozen Marine military police exited the vehicles behind him. They surrounded Governor Stein's residence.

The military police broke down the front door and swarmed through every entry point. They fanned out through the building with guns drawn. Every member of the staff was taken into custody before they confronted the governor in his office.

"Gallant, you'll never get away with this," shouted Stein as his hands were pulled behind him and cuffed.

Standing beside the Marines, Gallant said, "Governor Stein, I am placing you under arrest in the name of the United Planets for embezzlement, fraud, and wartime profiteering." He showed the governor a warrant with the charges and specifications.

Stein was apoplectic. He said, "President Neumann is my friend. He will have your head for this."

"I think not."

"I already sent him information about your violations of genetic engineering laws and your misbehavior as an officer. I recommended your removal. I'm confident that such an order will arrive very soon. You'll regret ever stepping foot on Charlie."

"I doubt that President Neumann will remain your friend once he reads my report on your embezzlement of his money," said Gallant. Then in a mocking voice, he added, "You shouldn't bite the hand that feeds you. You stole from NNR, Neumann's business. He's not going to take kindly to that. I've enclosed a complete accounting, as well as affidavits from Captain Wells and Captain Daux plus scores of other miners. No. It's you who'll regret stepping foot on Charlie."

Stein stamped his feet and said, "Those pretty buttons and bows on your chest may be enough payment for you. But I wanted more. I deserved more. And I was smart enough to get it."

"If you'll excuse me," said Gallant. "I have business to attend to that I am looking forward to, even more than this."

An arena-size dome was erect in the capital city of Charlie for the award ceremony. Military units and their families sat in the front, and civilians streamed in the stands behind them. The ceremony was to pay homage to the fallen and reward the valiant.

Gallant walked past the auditorium, where the preliminary formalities of the ceremony were beginning.

"Will Governor Stein be attending?" asked a spokesman.

"I'm afraid he had business elsewhere," said Gallant.

The opening comment rang out. "Good morning, ladies and gentlemen. Today, we honor members of the Space Force for their courage and sacrifice. Our families and friends join us in recognizing their contributions."

The people applauded loudly.

"We did it. We won. But it was a hard fight," said Gallant. "The price for our victory has been measured in the loss and suffering of those we loved."

Heads nodded.

"The battle is over. The struggle was long and grueling. But I can still see the teary eyes of our grieving warriors and their families. Now is our time for rejoicing."

Over the next hour, Gallant presented medals and awards to the deserving women and men.

At one point, Gallant said, "Now, I have a presentation that I find exceptionally satisfying. These two young people researched alien technology and provided information essential to our success. They gave our warriors the tools they needed to prevail." He picked up the medals and said, "Kate Mahoney and Daniel Logan, step forward."

As he draped the ribbons over their heads, he smiled his broadest grin. "Without your creative genius, we could have never defeated the Great Ship. I'm proud of you."

Kate blushed, and Logan grinned.

"With the loss of their last Great Ship, the Chameleon are a spent force. They are effectively out of the war," said Gallant. "And because we've successfully beaten the Titan fleet in open combat yet again, I am confident that we will finish this war soon."

Gallant waved his hand toward the governor's empty chair. He said, "Those who dismissed the courage of others and sought their own profit, have reaped their just reward. Those who referred to our ribbons and medals as 'buttons and bows' never understood that these are not a payment. They are a reminder, a reminder of who we are and how we serve a cause greater than ourselves."

He pointed to the stands. "To the families and friends of the men and women in the armed services, thank you for your support."

Then Henry Gallant spread his arms wide and said, "For those who have ever worn the uniform, ...

THANK YOU FOR YOUR SERVICE."

- the end. -

FROM THE AUTHOR

I would be very grateful if you could HELP me keep the Henry Gallant series alive by posting a supportive review on the first book of the series, Midshipman Henry Gallant.

This will allow me to write more Henry Gallant stories.

Thank you for your kind consideration.

H. Peter Alesso

Now available in Pre-order:

Rear Admiral Henry Gallant

The enemy aliens sued for peace . . . but they lied!

To Humanity's shock and horror, the Titans launched a surprise attack on the Solar System. They devastated the United Planet's Home Fleet.

Henry Gallant's Task Force 34 is all that stood between them and Earth.

At home, Alaina wants to start a family. Forcing Gallant to assess if he is a Natural "superman" or a disappointment to one and all.

Printed in Great Britain
by Amazon

46364059R00138